Tales from Another Time

A short story collection

Kian Ash

Tales from Another Time
A Maestrowork Book

Copyright © 2018 Kian Ash

ISBN ISBN-13: 978-0998671918

ISBN-10: 0-998671916

Published by Maestrowork, California
Manufactured in the United States of America

CONTENTS

MAKING UP FOR LOST TIME

It would take about fifteen milliseconds to for the bullet to travel and puncture the skull and destroy the brain tissues. After calibrating the instruments, I sat quietly next to a thick elm tree. The soft light filtered through the layers of foliage, reminding me of the day Nora and I first met at Kingsley Park. I'd missed her. I glanced at my watch: two minutes and twenty seconds to go before entering the no-change zone.

I peered out and studied the target. Sandy hair and a stocky build, the man a dozen meters away was only thirty-three years old. Whatever prompted him to come here, out in the woods, I'd likely never know. The only thing I'd have to make sure was that he'd be dead when it was over. A single bullet in the head. Gilliam was very specific about that.

Fifteen seconds to go. I lifted the gun and aimed. I'm ready.

It took 15.23462 milliseconds for the bullet to travel and puncture the skull and destroy the brain tissues. I'd made sure of that, made sure all the data had been verified and the calculation was correct and the site had been set up to specifications. I was dying to go home.

My wristband vibrated, and I pressed the button on the sync unit. I stared at the man's still body and, oddly, didn't feel a thing. I didn't know this man or his family, and his death wouldn't affect me at all. By tomorrow the police would find him and it'd be business as usual. Nobody would know I'd been here. I wasn't too concerned about all that, to be honest. What I was concerned about, though, was that Gilliam and I got exactly what we needed and got out of here in time.

Gilliam was already waiting at the rendezvous point by the river, his gray, unkempt hair flopping all over his weathered face. He summoned me by his signature flick of a hand. I nodded and snapped my pack onto the calibrator. He examined the data and eventually cracked a smile, his teeth unusually white against his beard tinted by the late afternoon sun.

"Good job, Dean," he said, absently polishing the polymeric barrel of his gun with a corner of his shirt. "Just one more and we can go home."

"Really. I thought this would never end."

"It's not so bad here."

"Well, it wasn't until I lost the damn tracker. I'm so sorry. I thought we would never catch up."

"Yes, it's all your fault." He laughed. "That was the fourth time you apologized, son. Thank goodness we didn't lose our guns. Life is an adventure, not a guided tour. Besides, I like it here. It's been a long time." He pointed at the stone bridge a couple hundred meters from us. "I remember that very well. A lot has changed since."

"You're so nostalgic. Not that I really care. I don't know this place."

"But you did enjoy yourself, right?" he said.

My grin must have given me away. "Yeah. I've learned a lot."

"That's good." He glanced at his GPS. "Let's get out of here before someone sees us."

After we crossed the bridge, we chose an obscure trail off the main road, through the woods and away from town. Gilliam knew where he was going; I'd always trusted him. We'd walked for about an hour, and I started to worry about the schedule. I just wanted to see Nora again -- She wouldn't even realize I was gone at all, but to me, it had been too long.

How long? Well, Gilliam and I had been here for three days, gathering information and studying our targets and the effects of the experiment. The expedition had gone very well, and he was pleased. We filled three teradiscs of data, enough to continue our work for another six months until our next expedition.

Then there was the damn Harvey's Tavern in Gainesville. We'd been very careful, trying not to be seen, but someone recognized Gilliam. We had to make a run for it, and I lost one of the trackers to the river. We could deal without one tracker, but we needed the exact sequential factors to go home. After the calibration, Gilliam confirmed that we'd lost a total of close to 38.23 units. Fortunately, he came prepared. He had the manifests and knew exactly where we could make up for the lost time, though we had to see to it that a few people died first.

The first was Mr. Durkowsky in South County. That one was easy. It didn't faze me at all, but I didn't realize Janet Collins would be so difficult. Too gruesome for me. My hands still shook thinking about the way she'd died. So I told Gilliam we should split up; he would go to Kent for the twins, and I would take care of the guy in the woods. Gilliam took a good look at me and agreed: I was ready to go solo.

Now, I stare ahead. Just one more job before we could go home.

"So," Gilliam said, "how did it go with the man in the woods?"

"It was okay. The worst part was watching him. It wasn't easy."

"You don't have to watch, you know. All you have to do is set everything up, and you can just walk away."

"I know. I just didn't trust myself, I suppose. After the tracker incident, I didn't want to screw up again." I tugged at the gun strapped around my shoulder. "What was his name, anyway?"

"Uh, Ron. Ron Davis."

"Did you know him?"

"Not really. He was a friend of my dad's. We went to his house once or twice, when I was much younger. Then he became kind of a drifter."

"It was a shame he had to die."

"He didn't have to die," Gilliam said. "He had a choice."

"You know what I mean."

He stopped and turned to me, and I knew from his dead stare that he was going to give me a lecture. I was right.

"Son, there was nothing you could do to stop it. He died, and that's it. Fine. The End. We just helped ourselves a little. I wish there were a better way, but you know our equipment only works on humans. And we're doing them a favor, actually."

"Yeah, I know… So, how did you do?"

"The twins? It wasn't pretty, but it netted us twenty-one full units. It was a slow death."

I whistled. "Twenty-one? That's great. So, we only need, what, four more?"

"Just about…" Gilliam turned and kept walking. "Let's go. We don't have much time."

I grinned, amused by the irony. No, we don't, but we are going to make some time.

"You haven't told me where we're going," I said.

He didn't say anything. The sun was setting behind us and we had got to leave these woods before dark.

"So, what is going on with this one?" I said.

"You don't want to know."

"Why? Is it nasty, like with Janet Collins?"

"No."

"What is it, then?"

He marched on in silence, dry leaves rustling under his feet.

"Doc?"

"It involves a child."

I dragged my feet on the dirt and stopped walking. I shouldn't feel anything about any of these people. I hadn't. But a child? My throat tightened. "How? And where?"

3

"Don't worry." Gilliam flicked his hand at me while trekking down the trail ahead of us. "It's totally isolated. Nobody will see us."

"That's not what I asked."

"And I said, don't worry."

"Isn't there anyone else?"

"I'm afraid not, Dean. That's our last and only target. I ran through the manifests, twice, already. And without this, we can't go home. We're running out of time."

Gilliam marched on without looking back. He was right; we were running out of time. I had no choice but to follow him closely.

The sun had been gone for about fifteen minutes. Gilliam and I stood under a large tree, studying the few specks of light at a distance against the darkening sky. The pasture smelled of dung, grass, and damp soil. I crinkled my nose. He shook his head and smirked. There wasn't a single country bone in this city boy, and Gilliam didn't seem impressed.

I strapped my gun tight against my back and followed him down the meadow toward the lights. I stepped on something squishy, felt nauseated by a pungent odor, but I didn't want to think about what it was – the only thing in my mind now was to finish the job and get the hell out of here.

As we neared the structure, we hunkered down and hid behind a bale of hay on a slight slope. Straight ahead stood an old farmhouse, only a few yellow bulbs illuminating its door and pale walls. I caught Gilliam stealing a glance at me before he looked ahead again. He wasn't staring at the house. I followed his gaze and saw the dark mass beyond the asphalt roof. He was sizing up the large barn at the back of the house. I stared at the barn again. I know this place. All right, I'd never been here before – I'd never even left the city before now – but I knew this place. I'd seen this house and the barn behind it before. Somewhere. But I couldn't put my finger on it.

"What is this place?" I whispered. Gilliam didn't answer. I raised my voice. "What is this place?"

"Just an old farmhouse, in the middle of nowhere."

An engine sputtered in a distance and a set of headlights shone our way. Gilliam and I ducked and crouched lower behind the hay, and we both peeked out from the side. A rusty blue pickup pulled up the gravel driveway to the farmhouse. The engine fell silent after a final stutter. A young woman stepped out of the house and turned to lock the door. She ran toward the truck and leaned in the passenger's side window, then laughed and pulled the door open and hopped in. Her laughter lingered in the air as the truck pulled away.

The lone bulb above the porch taunted me.

"I can't do this," I said.

"Then you wait here. I'll finish and come get you."

"How long?"

Gilliam looked at his watch. "Fifteen minutes."

"Are you sure—"

"Dean, don't make me repeat myself. You know exactly what we're doing and there's no other way. The cops are going to find Janet Collins in about an hour. Now, just wait here. I have a job to do and I'll be back in fifteen minutes."

The grass felt damp on my ass. I stared at the house, and in my mind, I went over everything that had to happen in the next few minutes, all the steps, the precision, and the result. I shouldn't care, but there was something familiar about this house. I know this place.

Then I remembered the photographs in my mother's attic. It took me only two seconds to realize what it meant.

"No."

I stood. The rush of blood in my head made me dizzy and I steadied myself on the bale. It gave way and I stepped aside, watching it tip over with a thud. I glanced at the yellow bulbs again, knowing what would happen when the young woman returned.

I hadn't recognized her before, but now her identity was clear to me. My mother. With her hair pulled up and tied in a ponytail, she'd looked beautiful in her bright flower dress. I'd forgotten how young she used to be; hell, she'd forgotten how young she used to be. But she remembered how quickly she had to grow up in 2008. Right now, ten years before I was to be born.

I didn't know much about Uncle Nate. My mother seldom talked about him, and when she did, it was always a passing comment about a nursery rhyme her baby brother used to hum or the way he would take a bite of his oatmeal and throw the bowl across the room and she would have to wipe everything up. But mostly, Nate was a ghost, a name my mother stopped saying a long time ago.

Did Gilliam know?

I tugged at my gun and approached the barn. Faint light seeped through the gaps between the wood planks. I leaned against the door, spooked by the silence. I could only imagine what was going on in there: Gilliam waiting in a dark corner, aiming his gun at the three-year-old. He was right – it would be a mercy, and the child would not suffer a bit; the ordeal for him would last only a fraction of a second, and then it would be over.

And my mother would be devastated and riddled with guilt for the rest of her life. It would nearly ruin her. One failed marriage after another. A lifetime of regrets.

It was inevitable. It had already happened.

But I couldn't let it happen again.

I pushed open the door and stepped inside the barn. Gilliam had his arms around a boy, with frizzy blond hair, slumping over the wall of a well. Gilliam looked up, his eyes widening as he stared at me.

"Get out," he yelled.

"What are you doing?"

"Get out."

I stepped forward. "Put the child down."

"Get out, Dean. I mean it. We don't have much time."

"There must be another way. We can find someone else."

"You really don't get it. I don't have a choice."

I noticed the child wasn't moving. "What have you done to him? Is he dead?"

"You know we need him alive. I just stunned him."

"Oh God, you've gone mad. You're actually going to murder him."

"He was already dead."

"He is still alive now." I took another step forward and realized something. "Why did you – it's not supposed to happen this way. It was supposed to be an explosion."

Gilliam put the child down and squinted at me. "How did you know?"

"My mother told me."

"Your mother? Who in the hell—"

"Becky Rainer."

"Becky... I'll be damned." Gilliam stared me down. "You're Becky's son? I should have recognized those eyes. But... I thought she married that bastard, Greenfield."

"She did. That bastard left her way before I was born."

"Well, well, what a small world, then. I can't believe you've worked with me for four years and I had no idea."

"You still haven't told me what you were doing with the child."

"Your Uncle Nate must die."

And this time, I knew what he meant. "You planned this."

He sneered. "Don't be ridiculous, Dean. How could I have planned something that already happened?"

"Then tell me." I glanced at his hands. "Why are you wearing gloves?"

"Dean." He took a step toward me. "The fact that we're here, having this conversation, postponing the inevitable, we may already have changed something and created a paradox. You know damn well Nate Rainer has to die tonight, and through his death, we can go home, and nothing would change in our universe. Don't let your sentimentality cloud your judgment. You're a bright man. Use your brain." He flicked his hand at me. "Besides, you don't even know him."

I looked at the child again. "You're not telling me everything. Something is not right. Why weren't you waiting in a corner like you—"

Before I knew it, Gilliam knocked me down on my back. He grabbed my gun and pushed the barrel under my chin, pressed hard and pinned me. His whole body weighed on me, his thick arm crushing down on my chest.

"I have no choice," he said.

I gasped for air. He pushed the barrel harder and I choked. He eased up but continued to lean his weight on me.

"When I came in, I didn't see him," he said. "He should have already got out of the house through the back door, wandered to the barn and stood by the well, just as the manifest said he would. But he wasn't there. He was still inside the damn house, sleeping. That's when I realized something. It was so simple, I almost laughed at myself for being so blind for so many years."

He turned me over. I struggled but he pushed my arms against my back. I felt his knees pressing hard on me, his hand firmly on my shoulder.

"Dean, my boy, Becky Rainer's son." He laughed, a sinister sound I'd never heard before. "For almost forty years I've thought that luck was on my side, that your mother should suffer from this horrible fate, that her only brother would burn to a crisp with her father's barn because she was so damn happy to sneak out and fuck Jessie Greenfield. She broke my heart. Ah, yes, Dean. Your mother, she had the most beautiful lips. The cruelest, most torturous, most unfaithful lips. When I heard the news about her brother, I knew it was karma. It was justice. The bitch had it coming."

"Fuck you."

He pushed my shoulder hard against the ground. I groaned. "When I didn't see your precious baby uncle standing by the well, I knew immediately. You see, time is circular. Everything already happened. What we did yesterday, or today, has already happened and is happening again. I am – I was the one who made this and is making this happen

7

now. I just had no idea that you would be Becky's son." He snickered. "This is too rich. I can't ask for a better ripple effect."

"It doesn't have to happen."

"Of course, it does. It already did. We can't change the past because we are the past. I can write twenty papers on this."

"Gilliam, listen to me, we can walk out of here…"

"And then what? Be stuck here forever? And create a paradox? You still don't get it. I've already told you it is the only option. There is no other way. And your mother deserves this."

"Gilliam—"

A sharp pain stung my back and everything turned black.

I jerked awake to the foulest smell. An immense headache paralyzed me, and I lay on my side, trying to suppress a gag reflex. A wall of hay pressed on my face, and the fumes of dung filled my nostrils. I gagged, foul liquid dripping down my jaw. I gagged and vomited again. Then I panicked. How long have I been out? I tossed over and pushed myself up. Gilliam must have dragged me out to the back of the barn after he'd stunned me. I scrambled up on my feet, felt queasy, steadied myself, and looked at my watch. I'd been out for a few minutes. Gilliam must still be inside doing – Oh God, I have to stop him.

I searched the ground and found a pile of bricks next to a trench. Holding one in each hand, I dashed to the barn's door and peeked in. Gilliam was standing by the well with his back to me. The boy had disappeared. This isn't good.

I slipped inside and inched toward him as quietly as I could. Gilliam leaned forward over the well, as though he was looking in. Has he drowned the boy? My stomach tightened as I lifted the brick in my hand and threw it. Missed. Gilliam turned immediately. I shifted the other brick to my right hand and threw again. It smacked him in the face and the force knocked him on his back, his head hitting the pulley. He groaned, his nose a bloody mess. I picked up a shovel by a barrel and went after him. The shovel crushed into his head. He rolled over on his side and slid off the well.

I looked over and saw what Gilliam had done. He'd tied the boy with a thick rope onto the top of the windlass. I shone a flashlight inside the well and my eyes followed another rope down the hole. What devious plan he had with the contraption he'd assembled in a bucket about six or seven meters down. The whiffs of natural gas confirmed it.

For a second, returning little Nate to the house seemed like a great idea. But then what? Gilliam and I would still be stuck here. Worse, I would have changed everything, including my own existence. I understood Gilliam better than anyone else: it had to happen.

Nate Rainer must die.

As mad as he was, Gilliam was a genius, and the knowledge of his scheme sent sharp shivers through me. His intention was clear. He was determined to go home.

Without me.

I leaned over him and pressed my fingers on his neck. His pulse was steady but his breath shallow. I needed him alive. What I had to do is to follow his exact plan, with only one alteration: Nate and I would take his place.

After releasing the boy, I carried Gilliam to the well and propped him over the top of the windlass. With my packs strapped to my chest, I tied the rope around my waist and secured the other end to the pole. I lifted the boy and carried him over my shoulder. Sitting on the edge of the well, I pushed my legs against the inside wall and started to lower myself into the hole by pulling on the rope. I missed my footing and almost lost my balance, wrapped an arm around the boy, my other hand pushing against the wall. Eventually, I made it to the bottom, the water waist deep and cold. Over the well's opening, Gilliam's still body slumped over the windlass, his torso and arms forming a big cross. A perfect position.

In my mind, I went through all the steps, and what had happened today. It was time to initiate the return jump.

After I'd lost one of the trackers, we had to create the extra temporal anchors to collaborate the jump. What we did was use the isolated events that had already been predetermined – events that we knew had already happened. The anchors would have had no effects on the surrounding events; but we had to determine, with absolute certainty, that the calculation was correct, and that we only took exactly what we needed.

We stole time.

No one would miss a thing. Nothing would change. Our field equipment was designed for human DNA signatures only, for they were the most precise and identifiable targets. The deaths were perfect. Gilliam knew exactly where to look for them because he already knew all about this day. We were in his past, and he had the manifests: Frank Durkowsky drowned when he fell off his boat; Janet Collins was beheaded and her body mangled when her car crashed in the mountains; the twins died in a gas leak. And Ron Davis shot himself in the head, deep in the woods. I'd made sure I'd captured the units with the quantum gun immediately after Davis pulled the trigger.

Nate's death would have completed the calibration. Nate was supposed to die in an explosion and a fire so ferocious that everything in and around the barn would be incinerated, leaving only ashes and melted metals, except for the hole in the ground.

Now I knew who had created the explosion.

I grabbed the bucket in which Gilliam had constructed the mechanism using both our quantum guns. I clicked the switch on my pack to start the jump sequence. All the anchors had been properly set up, and Gilliam had already reversed one of the guns. I set my pack to 4.3 units, then increased the count by 0.06326 until I heard a click, signaling the complete calibration. I synchronized the guns and pointed both at Gilliam. Right at the moment of the jump, the reversed gun would fire and everything would be over in less than a second.

I looked up at Gilliam again. His hand twitched.

Twitched again.

I only had one chance to do it right.

My wristband vibrated. It was time to go.

***

After dinner, Nora went for a walk with the terrier. Mom and I grabbed our cups of decaf and retreated to the back porch.

"Nora's a smart girl," Mom said, settling in her lounger.

"She is," I said, glancing at her wrinkled face. Age hadn't been kind to her. "So, fire away."

She laughed. "I was just surprised by your visit. It's been six years, Dean."

"I know. I'm sorry."

We sipped our coffee. I glanced up and studied the faint light above the porch, and thought about the past eleven months, after the "Project T accident." Nora knew everything, everything I had and hadn't done, and she encouraged me to settle everything.

"So, my dear, tell me about you and Nora," Mom said.

"If you're asking me about marriage, we will, some day. But right now we both have so much going on in our lives, and that's why we are here."

"I'm not sure I understand."

"Mom, let's go upstairs. I'll explain."

We put down our cups and went back inside. The smallness of the house and the clutter reminded me my father's death had been tough on her, too. She had a hard life, and I hadn't done anything to change that. I couldn't. Whatever happened happened. In fact, I was the cause of her misery. Guilt had found a way back to me. I had to fix this. I had to.

We entered the small bedroom at the end of the hall. Under the blue blanket, the boy lay still and his breaths were light. I pulled up a chair and sat next to the bed, then reached over and petted his hair.

"He's a beautiful boy," my mother whispered.

"Do you think you can love him?"

"Of course, Dean. He's your son. I'm hurt that you didn't tell me..."

"I'm sorry. But Nora and I would like to make it up to you."

"What do you mean?"

"Mom," I said. "Nora and I are going to South America for a while, and we talked about this. We'd love for you to take Etan."

"You can take him with you."

"Of course, we can, but Mom, I'd like for Etan to live with you for a while. It's time for you and him to know each other. Would you like that?"

I turned and held her hands, feeling them quaking in my touch.

"Would you like that?"

From the warm glints in my mother's eyes, I knew the answer.

BETTER SAFE THAN SORRY

Jo went over her gear once more, making sure she had everything she needed: ropes, chloroform, nets, flashlight, knives...and 20 cc. of tranquilizer. She sipped her cold coffee and then loaded her pack with two canisters of tear gas.

Matt studied her, acting concerned but amused at the same time. "Are you sure you need all that stuff?"

"Better safe than sorry."

"Do you have to go tonight?"

"Matt, I did my research. And Seth—"

"Ah, Seth, the cute sheriff."

Jo laughed and brushed a strand of hair from her face. "Don't tell me you're still jealous. Anyway, Seth just wanted us to be ready. The animal is vicious."

"That's the part of your job I don't like."

"But I do." Jo came over and kissed him on the forehead. "Not everyone likes a desk job."

"Hey." He pinched her on the ass.

She slapped his hand and smiled. "I gotta go."

With her backpack strapped to her shoulder, she headed out the door.

"Jo," Matt called.

She looked back and saw the seriousness in his green eyes.

"Do you have that special serum I gave you?"

"Yup, Doc. The syringes are good to go."

"Okay. Better safe than sorry, right?"

She smiled at him and disappeared out the door.

***

Seth Collins was down at the riverbank when Jo pulled her Jeep up next to his patrol car. Seth waved at her, and she went down to join him.

"Good evening, Ms. Cain."

"What's up?" she asked.

"There was a report of disturbance earlier this afternoon."

"But you said--"

"Yeah, I know, better safe than sorry, right?" He grinned. He pointed the flashlight at the muddy patch next to his feet. "You see these tracks? What do you think?"

Jo crouched down and took a close look. About two dozens of footprints in the mud, forming a few haphazard circles. She imagined there were possibly more, already washed away by the tide.

"These belong to the same animal. An animal," Jo said. "But not *the* animal."

"And you're saying?" Seth sounded somewhat disappointed.

"These are wolf prints all right, but we're not looking for a wolf, are we?"

Seth frowned.

"I don't know," Jo said. "I'm just telling you what I think." She stood and surveyed the ground around them. "A wolf was here this afternoon, and it seemed to be distraught, lost. See these circles? Seems like it's been pacing and circling, panicked about something."

"Interesting."

Jo stared at the river and sighed. "This is just crazy."

"What is?"

"Looking for it."

"I'm just following your expert opinions."

"I know what I said. It's just so, you know, *X-Files*."

Seth laughed. "Jo, in my line of work, I've seen many strange, bizarre things. But, I have to admit--"

She shook her head. "I don't think we're going to find whatever it is here."

"Okay. Sorry to have asked you *out*," he said, a deliberate pause, "here."

Jo smiled. She didn't mind a little flirtation with her tall, dark and handsome ex-boyfriend, even though her heart belonged to Matt now.

"I'm going back to the pound," she said. "If anything comes up, call me or look me up."

Seth winked at her. "You bet. You'll be the first to know."

***

On her way back, up the dirt road, Jo kept thinking about the *animal*. The eyes she saw that night.

That night. She'd thought perhaps an animal had gotten loose at the pound. She didn't remember exactly what had happened, only that the stench had been nauseating when she entered the building: animal feces mixed with blood and guts, the same revolting slaughterhouse stench she'd grown up with.

Then something had knocked her over, and in a blink, she saw those piercing pale yellow eyes in a corner staring back at her. She heard the snarls, so close and urgent.

Everything after that had been a blank wall until she woke up in a hospital bed, bandages all over her body. Her boyfriend, the burly Dr. Matt Campbell had stood by her side, his eyes tender, concerned and guilty-looking.

Matt told her that he'd gone to the pound to look for her when she hadn't come home for dinner. He'd seen something escape through the broken backdoor.

The pound was a shambles as if a tornado had whipped through it. Two Labs and a German Shepherd had been killed that night. Ripped to pieces, actually, their guts spilled all over the place.

Seth Collins told her a wolf must have entered the premises, and she was lucky to be alive. She knew she wasn't lucky. Matt must have saved her life by frightening the animal, somehow.

When Seth showed her the photographs of the scene, she knew something wasn't right. No wolf could have done it. And the prints...

Ridiculous. She'd laughed at the absurdity of the idea.

***

Jo arrived at the pound and parked the Jeep near the entrance. The sky was dark, and the air smelled like rain. The full moon threatened to break out from the heavy clouds.

She had an uneasy feeling about this place, yet something compelled her to come here. She checked her gear again. *Better safe than sorry.* That had become her favorite motto.

Jo took a photo from her pocket and studied the prints again. The claw marks looked like those of a wolf's, no doubt, but the paws were simply too large. Too long. The same shape of a human foot. And only the back paws, never the front.

The animal walked upright.

***

From the corner of her eye, Jo saw Matt's Volkswagen parked in the spot next to the dumpster. She jerked when she saw a shadow whisk by.

"Matt?" she shouted. Her voice was swallowed by the void. No one answered. *I must be seeing things,* she thought.

When she entered the building, Jo sensed something foul. The stench. She caught a whiff again. The animals were yelping and barking.

Her heart was thumping fast. She held her breath and swiftly unbuckled her pack. She reached for the tranquilizer gun.

She heard something fall behind her.

"Matt?" She turned.

She saw those eyes again.

A chill went up her spine.

In the glass door of a darkened office, she stared at herself.

Her pale yellow eyes stared back.

She breathed hard, her chest swollen with heat and her mind fogged with terror. Only for a second. Then a sudden lust for blood consumed her.

She heard the hapless creatures in the back. She breathed hard, and smelled that stench again: fur wet with feces, urine, saliva. The preys'. Her own. She was losing her mind, a savage desire sucking her in.

The room looked so clear and wide. Out the window, the full moon had broken free. It was calling her.

She pushed through the steel door, sniffing out preys. A Siberian Husky lay curled up in a corner cage, its silver-black fur stiffened with fear. She leapt. Landed by the cage. The husky backed up against the bars and whimpered. She rattled the cage, her claws scratching the steel, saliva flooding her jaw.

"Stop!"

She snarled and turned.

A man stood by the door with his arms extended, aiming a tranquilizer gun at her. He looked familiar.

She howled.

Pounced.

The man fired, but the dart missed its target. She landed on him, her claws dug deep into his shoulders. He let out a shrill cry and sank to the ground. He closed his eyes as she pinned him.

She pushed her head against him, sniffing his neck. That strong, raw, unspoiled scent of a male. One bite and that neck would snap in half. She would taste that blood, his flesh so sweet in her throat.

Instead, she stuck out her tongue and ran it along his face.

***

Boom!

A searing pain in her right shoulder jolted her. She snarled and pulled her claws out of the man's body. She turned and leapt.

Boom!

Another shot was fired, but it missed her. She crouched down and became the hunter herself.

She saw another familiar face. Her jaws clamped down and bones crunched. The scream in her ears turned her to ecstasy. She chomped again, and again, and again, her eyes misted with blood. Her claws tore deep in the soft clumps of flesh, crushing the bones around them, digging, mashing, their slushy sounds exciting her.

She feasted. When she was done, her fangs sank into the hairy skull and lifted it. An eyeball popped out of a socket.

Suddenly she felt a jab on her neck. She dropped the head and hissed. She turned and saw the window; the moon outside was being eaten by the gathering scuds.

A sudden calmness washed over her, an undercurrent of release. Her vision becoming blurry, and she searched for her assailant and found the man slouching over a steel table, a syringe in his hand, blood soaking through his shirt.

Matt.

"Easy now," he said. "It'll be over soon. Easy."

She crawled toward him, her limbs going weak. Another five feet, and she slumped onto the ground. She could move no more.

Matt approached and crouched next to her, then wrapped an arm around her head.

"Easy."

His eyes darted across the room at the carcass she had left scattered. His face remained calm, reassuring. The same tender, concerned, yet guilty look.

"Seth is dead," he said. Then he smiled. "That fool."

He cradled her head with one arm, then took a syringe from his pocket with the other hand. "One more. Just one more."

He stuck the needle in her arm.

"It'll be over soon. I promise."

He kissed her on the forehead.

And she saw his eyes.

Pale yellow.

He grinned and kissed her once more.

MASTERPIECE

Jerald took a long drag of his Marlboro. This last Thursday of February reminded Jerald of how much he hated winter. Nothing was more miserable than a blocked writer in New York in the depth of a snowstorm.

It'd been three months now, and Jerald was getting nothing. Nada. The writer's block was the worst he'd ever experienced, and not much could unclog it. Jerald's once-prolific career had culminated to a halt from a slow death since the lukewarm reception to his last novel, *The Psychosis Prophecy*. For two years, Jerald had come up with half a dozen ideas he thought would really rock the world and propel him from the mid-list to international fame. He had been working on his latest idea for the past eight months, but now the mental constipation had caught up with him.

His agent, Tucker, called him almost every day asking for progress. Tucker was under pressure, too, from the publishers. The only way Tucker could make money was when Jerald got something published. Anything, even a short story. Jerald knew very well how the business worked, but he always argued he was no Stephen King; he simply couldn't force his process.

He was better than Stephen Fucking King.

He exhaled and rubbed his hands together. Like it or not, he needed to add some words to the blank document. He started to type...

It was a dark and stormy night.

Jerald chuckled. It had come to this, a self-mockery that only exemplified the deflated spirit this former NOE winner once possessed. He had been a young, promising, uncompromising writer; then the devil showed up at his doorsteps. He took the money and abandoned his grand dream of writing the great American novel that would cement his place in the history of literature. Instead, his mortgage had been paid off, and he had enough left over for his ex-wife.

Jerald lifted his arms and yawned. Enough already. He gave up. Outside, the blizzard raged on so he could not even take a walk. He went to the kitchen, made another pot of coffee, sank into his favorite chair and turned on the TV.

Watching infomercials had become one of his favorite pastimes. George Forman's grill looked rather good after the Thigh Master telethon. Suddenly Jerald wanted a burger, and it didn't matter what the doctor had said about his cholesterol. He got up from his chair and headed for the stove.

The double cheeseburger made him lazy, and what would be more satisfying than a long nap when it was freezing outside? Jerald crawled into bed--it was never made, for a reason.

Soon, he found himself walking in a forest lush with grand sequoias and redwoods. A thin mist painted everything with a soft blue hue. Jerald followed the river and came to a clearing, where an army of mushrooms awaited him...

When Jerald opened his eyes, he couldn't see anything. He lifted his arm and it weighed like a ton. Once he got his bearings and his vision returned, he glanced at the bright LED on the alarm clock. It was after ten in the evening--he must have slept for at least six or seven hours. He didn't remember ever sleeping so deeply and for so long; sleep had been a luxury for him. And the dream--he rarely dreamed in his whole life--was the most vivid thing. He couldn't remember the details except he was in a forest, and there was a castle. He remembered, though, it had been a good dream, and something exciting had happened. He was certain about that.

He got out of bed and outstretched his arms. The room was dark. His heart sank a little knowing he had yet again wasted another writing day and, worse, he had let slip a great story that could have been in his dream.

He slogged through the hallway into his office. The bright glow of the computer monitor cast odd shadows all over the walls. Bending over to turn off the machine, he noticed a stack of paper on his desk. *Strange.* He did not remember seeing it this afternoon.

Crisp edges, clean white sheets, dark courier font--years of experience told Jerald what it was. Yes, a typed manuscript. But whose? He almost never agreed to read anyone's manuscripts, not even those of his closest friends. He took a quick look and was astounded by the words on the title page:

THE KINGDOM OF CRON
By
Jerald U. Douglas

What? He didn't remember ever writing anything under that title, and he sure had not dug anything up from his drawers full of unpublished old crap.

Jerald took a seat in his swivel chair and leaned back, held the manuscript on his lap, and started flipping the pages. As he read on, he recognized his own style, the word choices, but not the actual writing, and definitely not the story or characters; it was as if his twin, if he had one, would have written it. Yet the story gripped him from the first sentence, and he kept turning the pages, and found himself lost in that strange, foreign land of epic fantasy. Then a rogue wave of revelation hit him hard, and he almost fell off his chair. The story! It was so familiar that he really did think he'd written it. Now he knew why. He had dreamed it all: the Forest of Renaé, the Mushroom King, the castle high on Mount Arus and, of course, the entire Kingdom of Cron. The Battle of Izzarc. The adventure on these pages took him back to his dream. The plot twisted and turned and had his jaw on the floor by the time he came to the two coveted words: THE END.

After he'd finished reading and recovered from the exquisite ending that'd broken his heart, he sat in his chair, speechless and spent, cold sweat running down his neck. He slumped, and then perked up as he realized what this all meant.

It was the best thing he had ever read. Correction: *written.* He had indeed written an epic. But how? Had he done this in his dream? He shook his head: *Impossible.* Even if he had written it in his sleep, it would have taken him days simply to type up the 500-page manuscript. He checked the pages again, smelled the paper, and slapped his cheeks a few times. It was real, all right.

Could this be a practical joke? Jerald shook his head: if it were, it would be a damn brilliant one.

Exasperated, Jerald called Tucker immediately.

"Jerry? It's late." Tucker growled.

"I know, I know. Tucker buddy, you wouldn't believe what just happened."

"What? If you've won the Powerball, you still owe me fifteen percent, you hear me?" Tucker chuckled.

"It's better than the lottery. I think I, yeah, I have written a masterpiece."

"Huh? You were just telling me yesterday that you'd got nothing."

"Right, right. I was, well, just being coy. I just finished it tonight."

"Really? Great. To be honest, it's got to be better than *Psychosis Prophecy.*"

"You bet. I'll express it to you first thing tomorrow."

"I can't wait. Good job, Jerry, I'm proud of you."

"Trust me, it's nothing like you've read from me before. Or anyone else."

"Gee, you must have had quite a breakthrough tonight. You sound like a completely different person than you were the past few months."

"You're looking at a Pulitzer, man."

"Well, send it over and let me take a look, and I'll let you know if it's a Pulitzer or a Bulldozer."

"Yup, first thing in the morning."

Jerald couldn't contain himself. He put the manuscript in a document box and placed it carefully on his desk. Just to be sure, he closed the door to his office and locked it.

A most gratifying day. He went into the kitchen and made himself another double cheeseburger. Still racking his brain on how on Earth he'd managed to create the manuscript seemingly from his lucid dream, he chomped on his cheeseburger and sipped from his glass of diet Coke. Had there been anything unusual that had happened? Something, other than the cheeseburgers, that he had eaten? What had brought on this spurt of mad creative genius?

He couldn't think of anything, no matter how hard he tried, and eventually he gave up. He walked back to the office and unlocked the door, peered in and made sure the box still sat on the desk like a present ready to be opened on Christmas day.

He kept doing that the whole night. He couldn't sleep.

The snow outside his bedroom windows was coming down thick. Bastard weather. He stretched his back and wrapped an arm over his shoulder, trying to scratch an itch just under the shoulder blade. He couldn't reach, so he slid off to the floor and rubbed his back against the edge of the bed. He hadn't slept a wink all night. Craving coffee, he sauntered to the office, and unlocked the door.

The box is still there. He opened it and double-checked the manuscript. Nothing seemed more real now.

He drank a strong pot of coffee, scoffed down a bowl of cereal, put on his thickest coat and rushed out of the house with the box under his arm. Fortunately, the FedEx drop box was only five blocks away. Fluffy white flakes blanketed his head, his coat. Everything. He was glad he wasn't the only idiot on the street, but this idiot was going to become very rich. Famous.

That night, Jerald had a nightmare. This time, he was transported to a foreign planet with an advanced army of super-intelligent aliens. Trapped in a floating cell, he banged on the metallic walls, and discovered some ancient writing near the base of the cell....

As expected, there was a message on his answering machine the following day when he got back from the grocer. Snow still thick on him, he took off a glove and pressed the "play" button.

"Jerry, call me." That was all Tucker had to say, and his voice didn't sound that happy.

That surprised Jerald. He had worked with Tucker for over fifteen years and through twenty-three books. Tucker and Jerald had always been on the same page. Granted, Tucker hadn't liked *The Psychosis Prophecy* but went ahead with it, and it turned out to be an almost-disaster. It was understandable, after that debacle and two more years without a new manuscript, that Tucker would be skeptical. And yet there was not a sliver of doubt in Jerald's mind that *The Kingdom of Cron* was the best thing he had ever written – if he could finally accept that he had written it. Jerald would bet his apartment, his entire savings, and his life on it.

He called Tucker immediately.

"Jerry," Tucker greeted him with hesitation. "Are you playing a joke on me?"

"What do you mean?"

"It was you who sent me the FedEx, right?"

"Right, I sent it first thing in the morning, express. Did you get it?"

"Of course I did."

"Did you read it?"

"Read what?"

"The manuscript. *The Kingdom of Cron*."

"*The Kingdom of Blanks* is more like it. Jerry, you sent me five hundred blank sheets of paper. Nice stock, and thank you. But where is the damn book?"

"What? I swear, it was all there."

"No, it's not. I'm telling you."

"I--I don't know. I swear to God I sent it to you this morning, and it didn't leave my desk all night."

"Did you double check it?"

"Of course I did. I'm not an idiot."

"Jerry," Tucker said. "Are you feeling okay?"

"Yes, why? Do you think I'm crazy?"

Tucker didn't say anything. Then he sighed. "Maybe you're just stressed out. I know you've been under a lot of pressure, from me and from everyone else. Maybe you should take a short break, go to the Bahamas or something. It'll do you some good."

"I don't need a stupid vacation. I'm telling you, it was right there and I sent it to you. It's the best thing I've ever written."

"Jerry..."

"You don't believe me? After fifteen years?"

"Yes, Jerry, I believe you. I do. And I hope you believe me when I say all I got here was five hundred pages of scrap paper."

"Someone must have made a switch."

"You mean someone stole your work?"

"That's what I mean."

"Listen, Jerry. I've been with you for fifteen years, and never once did anyone steal anything from you. Not even a paragraph. It just doesn't happen."

"This is different. It's a masterpiece, not the other crap."

"Jerry, listen to me--"

Jerald hung up on him. Tucker was being a jerk. What did he mean by five hundred blank sheets of scrap paper? Impossible. He knew what he'd read, and it was the best story he'd ever written.

Was it possible that someone had stolen the manuscript? If so, who? One of the writers in his circle? Raymond Bart, perhaps? He now wished he'd made a copy.

He went into his office to check the computer. Nothing. Not a trace. In fact, the words "It was a dark and stormy night" continued to stare at him.

Had it all been in his head? Was he delusional? No, he convinced himself. He knew what he'd read and he couldn't have made it up in his head. It was too real.

The Kingdom of Cron was real.

A thought went off in his head, and he wanted to make sure he wasn't crazy. He looked to the right of his computer. And there it was: another stack of paper sat neatly on the desk. He lunged forward and grabbed it, feeling the familiar texture of the 20 lb bond in his hands, the title page perfectly printed in Dark Courier:

PRISON WAR
By
Jerald U. Douglas

It was no mistake. The printed words were as dark as the story itself. As Jerald slumped and twitched in his chair, he read, savored every word, and let the alien world swallow him. When he came out of the other end, he couldn't see through the tears in his eyes. He was a changed man.

Prison War was a hundred times more potent and exquisite than *The Kingdom of Cron.*

More important, Jerald had begun to understand how the cogs and wheels turn in this latest bout of magical creations. His dreams, he realized, must have materialized into these masterpieces. Every word was perfect, every sentence sublime, and every page riveting. Jerry remembered what it had been like as a kid wanting to be the greatest writer in the world; but that dream had always eluded him. *Prison War* was his vindication.

The snow had eased up as Jerald stopped at the nearest Kinko's. He couldn't take another chance, and he had to prove that he wasn't delusional. He must have asked the clerk ten thousand times if she could see anything on those precious five hundred twenty-four pages, and he must have heard the word "yes" a million times. Not losing any momentum, he dropped the manuscript with the courier service and demanded that the package be delivered the same day. He couldn't take any chances.

And then he drank a lot of coffee. He waited.

As ten o'clock rolled around, the phone rang, and Jerald grabbed the receiver immediately.

"Tucker?"

"Jerry, my man," Tucker said. His cheerful voice calmed Jerald. "I got it."

"Did you read it?"

"Are you kidding? I devoured it. It's magnificent, man. I can't tell you how proud I am of you. And I'm sorry I doubted you before. This is the best thing in the world. But, I'm confused. This isn't *The Kingdom of Cron.*"

"This is better."

"How did you do it? It's humanly impossible."

"Why? What do you think I've been doing these past two years?"

"Oh, so you've been holding out? You couldn't even trust me enough to tell me?"

"I didn't want to jinx anything."

"Well, I'll tell you, this is a masterpiece, no doubt about it. I've got to send it to the editors immediately."

"Today?"

"Well, they'll have to go out tomorrow morning."

"This can't wait."

"Jerry, all is good. Trust me."

"No, no, you don't understand…"

"What don't I understand? Jerry, you've got to give me some time. Publishing is a very slow business, even for geniuses like you. It may be a few days before they'll read it. You simply can't rush them."

"I know," Jerald muttered. "How long?"

"I'll try to hurry them up, but this truly is magnificent, and I can't imagine them not jumping on it within the next few days."

"That's all I need to know."

"Don't worry, Jerry. All is good. Now, go get some rest. You sound scratchy. Go to bed."

Go to bed. That was exactly what Jerald couldn't do.

Now that he realized what was happening, he knew that once he went to bed, all would be lost. He couldn't take that chance. Not at all.

He made an extra strong pot of coffee, drank the whole thing, and sat in his swivel chair, waiting for the sun to come up.

Jerald awoke in a sheet of sweat. His fear had consumed him and he gasped for air as he opened his eyes, immediately reassured by the familiarity of his office walls. Disoriented, he glanced around and caught the blinking cursor on his computer monitor.

It was a dark and stormy night.

Had it been all a dream? He scurried off his chair and reached for the desk. There. A stack of paper. Then a terror tore through him: *no, no, no.* He fell off his chair, got up, and dashed toward the file cabinet. He pulled out the Kinko's box from the top drawer and opened it.

"NO!" he screamed. It was gone. The copy. Nothing but blank sheets of cheap Xerox paper.

He fell on the ground, and the papers in his hands scattered like broken wings. Once again, his masterpiece had disappeared completely, without a trace. All that was left was the confusion of whether he was indeed insane.

Sure, he could probably rewrite the whole thing from scratch, from the memory of what he'd read. It was, after all, his own creation even if it'd come from the deepest part of his subconscious mind and somehow manifested into a literary gem. There was no answer as to how it was possible, just that it had happened. His dreams were the ultimate machine of creation and a weapon of destruction. There was no way to control it.

Except for one thing.

Jerald remembered. He'd had another dream before he awoke soaking in sweat. That dream was the reason why *Prison War* had disappeared, but it also meant something else must have been created. He looked over to his desk, and let out of sigh when he saw the tall stack of paper next to his computer.

Jerald unplugged his phone, closed the blinds, grabbed the manuscript and sat in a corner. Alone. Nothing between him and the world his dream had created.

His despair turned into ecstasy as he flipped through the new manuscript. *Unforgiving Silence.* He promptly became part of that world--a world so similar to his own and yet so vastly different, where politics and religions and humanity had turned upside down and inside out; where men were animals and they hunted each other; where one man's madness turned the human race onto itself; where the redemption of men could only come if the last one on Earth would sacrifice himself for their legacy without a future.

Jerald sat in the corner for a long time--he couldn't tell how much time had passed. He didn't know if Tucker had tried to call, and he couldn't have cared less. He had *the* story of the millennium in his hands. There was no way he would let it go, not now, not ever. He must find a way to preserve it until the whole world had a chance to be enthralled, enlightened, and enriched by this gorgeousness.

That's how God wants it.

Jerald went to his computer and started retyping the manuscript into a document, word by word. Fifteen pages later, he changed his mind. He couldn't take any chances. What if it disappeared just as the photocopy had? What's to stop it from happening?

Instead, he pulled out a yellow legal pad and started transcribing the manuscript by hand. His writing turned fierce and mad, as the day grew long and his hand got tired. Fifty pages. Seventy-five pages. It would take him at least three days, nonstop, to transcribe the 150,000 words of genius. He took a break and made a pot of extra strong coffee, then went back to his desk and started transcribing again.

His eyes stinging, his fingers numb and his wrists limping over the stacks of paper on his desk, Jerald half-closed his eyes and nodded, not because he had finished, but because he hadn't slept for three days. He hadn't had time to eat or wash or go to the bathroom. Only coffee and the desire to preserve his masterpiece had sustained him. And yet he'd only finished two-thirds of the manuscript. Jerald dug his hands into his hair and pulled at the strands. He knew he couldn't go on like this any longer, and soon he would succumb, and he would dream again, and all would be lost once more. He couldn't let this happen. "The Greatest Writer of All Times." He could taste the glory on his tongue. There was no way he would let that slip through his fingers, now that he knew what he had accomplished, and what he had to preserve.

He looked at the neatly typed manuscript on the left, and his scribbling on the legal pads. The images started to blur, and he had no idea where he was or what he was writing. Nothing made sense anymore. He drank another cup of stale coffee, and the bitterness in his mouth sent him shivering. His throat tightened and his stomach convulsed. He was afraid he would start hallucinating. Not now, not ever, not when he'd only finished with two-thirds of the damn thing.

He couldn't let himself sleep. It was personal.

For as long as he didn't go to sleep, and as long as he didn't dream again, his masterpiece would stay, and the world would have a chance to weep and bow to his brilliance. And that was worth more than anything else in the world.

Anything.

He pulled out a clean sheet of paper, and he wrote:

Dear Tucker:

I'm sorry for all the troubles you have to go through, and I'm sorry that I won't be here to tell you exactly how regretful I am that this has to happen. Please know that I respect you and I have enjoyed the last fifteen years we've been together. You are not only my agent; you're my friend.

In case you're wondering, I am not insane. These past two years have been difficult on me, what with the disaster in my career, my son's death, my divorce. I knew all that. And I am grateful you've been there for me, through thick and thin. And I'm comforted to know that you will be here for me at the end.

That's why I'm leaving you this. I know by now you must be skeptical about what I tell you, but this is the truth. Read this manuscript, and you will understand why I must do this. And I'm confident that you will do the right thing with it.

Your dear friend,
Jerry

He cleared everything off his desk, turned off his computer, and placed the manuscript neatly at the center on the desk. He then placed the letter on top of the stack.

He got up from his chair and staggered toward the bedroom. The vision of his comfortable bed and the double layers of soft blankets confused him. He shook his head vigorously, trying to get rid of the images. As he regained his focus, he reminded himself what he had wanted. He needed something in the bedroom--something that would make him the greatest writer of all times.

He leaned over the bed, and the softness of the sheets seduced him. He bit his lip and shook his head. *No, no, no. I can't sleep. Never.* He reached for the nightstand and pulled open the drawer. There was something he needed.

He felt inside the drawer and his fingers touched a steel box, sending a sharp jolt through him. *Yes, that's it.* He grabbed the box, took it out and opened it. Inside, the steel barrel of the .35 looked breathtaking.

He could never sleep. He would never sleep. He knew that now. And there was only one way to make sure of that.

He unlocked the safety, lifted the gun to his head, felt the cold barrel pressing against his temple.

For glory.

At the police station, Tucker Corbin was still shaking when Detective Howell handed him a cup of coffee. Tucker almost spilled it as he thanked the detective.

"You all right?" Howell asked.

"Yeah...yeah, I'm okay."

"I need to ask you a few more questions, when you're ready."

"I'm ready."

"Are you sure?"

"Yeah." Tucker took a gulp from his cup. "I am."

"Mr. Corbin, if I understood correctly, you found Mr. Douglas this morning, at about ten o'clock," Howell said, checking his notes. Tucker nodded and sipped his coffee again. "What exactly happened?"

"Well, like I told the other officers, I hadn't heard from...from Jerry for a few days, so I got worried. He wouldn't answer his phone. After the blizzard was over, I came over to see him, to see if he was okay. I had a key--we were good friends. I took care of his fish when he went away."

"What made you think he wasn't okay? Was there anything that tipped you off?"

"He was acting very strange lately," Tucker explained. He went on telling the detective everything about his conversations with Jerald and the manuscripts.

"So," Howell said, "he was hallucinating when he sent you the blank pages. Do you know if he had a habit of using drugs?"

"No, Jerry doesn't--didn't even drink. He was a good guy. He just had a rough time these couple of years. And he wasn't hallucinating. I've read his book. He was telling the truth."

"Where is the book now?"

"I made copies and sent them to a few editors."

"And can these editors collaborate on this?"

"Well," Tucker said. "That's the thing. They called me and told me all they'd got was blank sheets of paper. But I swear I put them in the mail myself."

"So, you have no evidence to support your claim."

"No, sir. I'm afraid not."

"All right. But he did leave you a letter."

"He did. I believe you've got a copy."

"Got it."

"So, you think it's suicide?"

"I can't really say."

"What really happened then? Nobody told me anything."

"Somebody put a bullet in his head."

"Jesus."

"But he missed. The bullet got lodged in Douglas's lower brain."

Tucker sighed. "Did he suffer long?"

"No, he didn't. He was in a coma for just a couple of hours," Howell said. "Now, Mr. Corbin, can you tell us about the manuscript."

"I told you already."

"No, the other one. The one he left with his letter."

Tucker grimaced. "Oh, that manuscript."

"Can you explain it to me?"

"No, I can't."

"Why do you think Mr. Douglas left that for you, and what do you think he wanted you to do with it?"

"I honestly have no idea."

"Can you tell us what it is about?"

Tucker Corbin shifted his body in the chair. He strained his neck, squinted, and lowered his voice.

"Gibberish. Simply gibberish. Five hundred pages of mad gibberish, as if he'd typed the darn thing when he was in a..."

He sucked in a breath.

"Coma."

Lack of Character

It was barely ten in the morning and the day had already gone to shit for Clay Brinkley, owner of Clay's Book Store in historic downtown Cleveland. Clay sipped his cheap coffee and was extremely irritated by the absence of his niece, Sally. One day he was going to fire her, maybe the week before Christmas, so he could save the $300 holiday bonus. He took another sip from the mug, and realized he still had to close the month by the end of the day. *Crap.* The good thing, and the bad thing, was that customers were scarce. It was, after all, Monday morning. *Who buy books on Mondays?*

It didn't help that he just had the most annoying phone call in his life. Max Keller, the self-published writer, called again, about his absurd novel, *Edit or Die*, which he'd sent Clay two months ago. Clay had forgotten about it until Keller reminded him of the unpleasantness. He had only read three chapters and already got a sickening headache. The plot was absurd, to say the least, and gratuitous. There was no character development, no character depths at all -- they were all terrible, unlikable people. How did Keller dream up his characters? *Tripe*, Clay declared. *Pure Tripe.* No way would he give the book a space on one of the sixty-six shelves in his store. He had a reputation: his elite boutique bookstore was a landmark. Authors like Michael Chabon and Khaled Hosseini had graced this space. He had no time for hacks such as Max Keller.

Keller hadn't taken it well when Clay gave him his scathing conclusion this morning. Keller couldn't understand what Clay meant by words such as *crap*, *tripe*, and *garbage*. Keller couldn't understand why Clay refused to stock the book or host a book signing. After Clay tried to convince him that supporting local authors didn't mean supporting trash, Keller's voice changed. It was a cackle -- no, more like a croak -- as if Keller was cracking right beneath his pretend sophistication. Clay didn't remember the rest of the conversation. He did remember Keller's threat, something about living a nightmare over and over again.

What a tool.

Clay just laughed.

By five o'clock, Clay had finished with his paperwork. He'd sold on average a book an hour, and decided it was time to close the shop. He drove the beat-up Volvo to the nearby Kroger and got a bag of Chow Fun's favorite nibble-bits. All bacon. *Liar!* But the mutt loved this crap. Man's best friend, that much was true. Ever since Clay split with the wicked witch of the West Side, Chow Fun had been his loyal companion through thick and thin, through snow and rain, through joint pain and bad knees. The only thing Chow Fun ever demanded was his nibble-bits and a hearty rub-and-scratch under the chin. The slobbering beast wouldn't have it any other way.

Clay pulled up his driveway. The last dangling leaves on the scrawny maple had joined their decaying brothers across the patchy yard. He checked the mail: junk, junk and more junk. Tossed them all in the trash. At least the gas company didn't send their goddamn bill yet. Another thirty-cent rate hike? *Bastards.* Clay figured he would just burn the Christmas tree for warmth. Bah Humbug, indeed.

He opened the door and called for Chow Fun and listened for the pitter-patter of the beastly paws on the hardwood floor. The silence puzzled him. He called for the mutt again, and when the fur ball didn't greet him, he made a mental note: No nibble-bits tonight.

He started to unpack the grocery bag when he heard a loud croak. Damn frog, but this time of the year? Shouldn't most frogs be dead by now? It was just a flat hiccup of throaty groan. He put the Half & Half in the fridge and called for Chow Fun. *Where is the damn clown?* Must have passed out, exhausted from chasing his tail all day. No nibble-bits tomorrow morning either.

The two fingers of port wine calmed him. Right now, he could use a foot massage and a hot bath. Carrying the evening paper under his arm, he caught a muffin from a plate and took a big bite of its crusty top. The frogs croaked again. Then a sharp clank jolted the muffin from his hand. *What the hell?* The sun had barely set. Too early for raccoons; besides, they should all be dead by now, what with the Drano-laced bread crusts out on the back porch. He called the mutt again. Nothing.

He cursed under his breath, put down the paper, and looked out the window on the back door. Couldn't see anything, but the croaking got louder and it wasn't his imagination that they had become an army of bass trumpeters. He swore, swiped a pot and a ladle from the counter and sneaked out the door. The chill in the air startled him. He climbed the short steps to the deck, enshrouded by a fog of shadows, the croaking mere feet away from him. He reached for the switch of the porch light and flicked it on.

Hundreds of tiny black eyes stared at him. His legs buckled, and he took a step back. In the faint glow of the light, the frogs, each the size of his fist, huddled into a dark green mound of slimy flesh. Beneath the heap of moving amphibians lay a wet mass of fur.

Composing himself, Clay clanked the pot and shooed the frogs away. They wouldn't go. Then two hopped, and hopped again, toward his feet. He backed off, and three more leapt at him, their dark beady eyes blinking with their frenzied croaks. One landed on his shoe. He kicked and sent the wet lump into the umbrage. More came for him, and he swung the pot and ladle at them, missing, then hit one with a squashy thud, then missed again. He backed down the steps and grabbed the door handle, yanked the door open and slipped inside.

He called for Chow Fun again, but the mutt wouldn't answer. His stomach churned; the tip of his tongue turned bitter. *Is the mat of wet fur Chow Fun? Is he dead? What have the frogs done?* He peered out the window again. It was black as the Reaper's cloak. He reached for the phone and discovered the handset was gone. No way. It was there this morning. He remembered clearly that he had called his mother at seven, right there in the kitchen. Maybe the wicked witch was playing a trick on him, but she didn't have a key. He'd changed the locks three times already.

Besides, Nina loved Chow Fun. She wouldn't have killed him.

His chest tightened. Perhaps it was just a dead cat or raccoon, and he misplaced the handset after all. He turned on all the lights in the kitchen, then in the hallway. Chow Fun wasn't at his favorite spot near the fireplace, nor was he by the flowerpots in the living room.

He heard a loud thump above him.

There you are, you little bugger. He called for Chow Fun again but the mutt still wouldn't come. *No nibble-bits for you this damn week.* The frogs' croaks outside became ridiculously loud. He climbed up the stairs, each step a creaking breath squeezed out of a frog's belly. By the time he reached the landing, he froze.

Blood. Streaks of blood. Fresh blood still shiny and slick on the dark oak.

He stopped and listened, heard a thump again, apparently coming from the end of the corridor: the master bedroom, where he stowed his only gun under the bed. *Damn.* He slowly backed down the stairs, each creak making his heart beat faster, and then dashed toward the front door and pulled.

What the hell? The door wouldn't budge. He turned the locks and pulled again. Nothing. Someone must have bolted the door from the outside. His first thought was the wicked witch, but logic escaped him. Was she trying to scare him? Kill him? *What's the purpose of this?* He dashed back to the kitchen and pulled on the back door.

Locked.

Sweat dripped down his forehead and back. He shook. Something frightened him and it took him five seconds to realize what it was. Dead silence. The frogs had stopped croaking. His mind spun, trying to pull the threads together and make some sense out of everything.

Everything turned dark.

He leaned against the counter and felt for the light switch. Flick. Flick. Flick. Nothing. Then he heard the thump upstairs. Louder this time. *Thump.* Louder every time. He began to yell, but swallowed the words with a sinking lump in his chest. *The intruder, whoever he may be, can't see me either.* The thought flickered excitement, adrenaline now pumping through his veins. He hunkered down and reached for the top drawer next to him and felt the sharp edge of the cleaver pressing against his fingers. Grabbing the handle, he pulled the weapon close to his heart.

Thump. Thump. Thump.

The sounds traveled toward the stairway. In his mind, he conjured the floor plan of the house and mapped out his moves. If he inched close to the arched doorway down the hall, he could strike the intruder in the knee as he came down the stairs. He'd better hurry, though, before the intruder got down the stairs first.

He crawled toward the hallway, his teeth clamping down on the cleaver's handle. The thumps were directly above him now. Quickly he slid forward and felt for the narrow nook around the corner, a mere foot away from the bottom of the staircase.

He held on to the cleaver. Bit his lip. Stopped breathing.

Thump. Thump. Thump.

Then it stopped. All but silence.

He held his breath, the cleaver shaking in his hand. *Come on. Come down and meet Papa.* He held the cleaver out slightly, ready for his swing.

The frogs croaked again, jolting him, and he leaned forward onto the ground. He shook.

The frogs were now inside the house.

Above him.

How the Hell did they get in?

The thought barely registered when a sharp pain penetrated his left calf. He crawled forward, flipped over and swung the cleaver above him. He swung again, in the darkness where life became a concept and death a reality, where fears manifested as nightmares and pain turned real.

Another sharp, searing pain punctured his right thigh. He yelped, his voice shrill and trembling, as if it were someone else's. The deep, hot pain was all his. He dragged himself backward, up against a wall, his hands now drenched in his own blood.

Something grabbed onto his hair and pulled. He swung his arms above, and promptly felt them disappearing in the air. The pain squeezed him tight as his head was yanked backward, leaving him gagging in his own spit. He muttered a faint scream. Two wet globs landed in his mouth.

Frogs.

And then they were all over him.

Suddenly he remembered. Frogs. A man and his frogs.

The way the egocentric editor died in Max Keller's ridiculous, sadistic self-published novel, *Edit or Die*, only to find out, like a recurring nightmare, he would die again, and again, and again.

He barely mumbled the word *Max* when a wet mouth swallowed his face…

***

It was almost three in the afternoon and Sally couldn't contain her excitement. She had read the book twice already and loved every word. Ever since she had taken over the Book Store, after Clay had disappeared, and found Max Keller's novel in the back office, she had fallen in love with the twisted, bizarre tales the dark man had spun before her. She'd stocked every one of Max's books, and when the call came, she almost fainted.

Max Keller was having a signing at her goddamn store. Today.

He sure was a large man. She waited for Max to settle in before she approached him. Her voice cracked and she started to apologize.

"Mr. Keller," Sally muttered. "Would you sign my book, please?"

"Of course." He personalized the book for her, and his autograph was huge and bold. A cordial, humble man. Nothing like the sadistic, sick bastard she'd imagined him to be.

"Did you like the book?" he said with a grin.

"Yes, yes. Yes. I loved it. It's my favorite. Yes."

"What did you like about it?"

"Everything. It's so clever. Like, the cleaver part was totally awesome."

"Anything else?"

"Yeah, it's like, every time I read your books, it's different. I can't explain it. Like, the story just took on a life of its own and I forgot, like, what'd happened before. Everything was so fresh and new. Again and

33

again. Like, it's new every time. And the main character reminds me a lot of my old boss."

"Is that right?"

"Yeah. You know, my boss disappeared."

"Interesting."

"They never found out what happened to him," she whispered. "Anyway, your emotions are so raw, the fright so intense, like the characters are living through this stuff. Like in a nightmare or something. I can almost taste that fear."

"My characters do tend to do that. They make the story come alive."

"And they feel so real."

"Maybe they are."

" If there's only one criticism, Mr. Keller, it would be the ending. I didn't understand it. It doesn't seem to end. It kind of just, like, falls a bit flat."

"Flat?"

His lips parted, showing a perfect set of white teeth. He cleared his throat. Then a hearty laugh, almost a loud croak.

"Sally, right?" He smiled. "Say, would you like to be a character in my next book?"

MOTHER

I sat at one end of the long hall of the funeral parlor and nodded at the people who came to see my mother; they had the same obligatory, morose expression on their faces, none of which I recognized. The reporters paid their visits, and then they left, seemingly blissful with their little stories and snapshots of an expired film star, and perhaps a few of her ungrateful daughter. I hid my face under the hood of my white robe, not wanting to be noticed. People didn't stop coming and leaving; the gong and the chimes didn't stop ringing; the muffled chants of the Taoist monks didn't stop humming in my ears. The incense started to irritate my eyes, and I began to choke and sniffle and tear up. The spectators were most likely commentating on what a great performance I'd been giving. All I could think of was how the ceremonial bird and sweetmeat and fried pastry would go to waste. My mother would never have touched them.

Auntie Lau came over and sat next to me. She always reminded of one of those gnomes in my garden, only without the beard and pointy hat.

"How beautiful." She pointed at my mother's portrait and sighed. Her Cantonese soothed me. "She was beautiful then, and she is beautiful now. When we were young, oh, much younger than you are now, back in Suzhou when the sun roasted us like chicken smothered with our own thick oil, your mother and I would go to the reading class near the next village, where all the boys were. Our villages were partitioned by short stone walls, like a fortress, but anyone could climb over those walls. I was small and shy, but your mother was bold. One time, she whistled at a new boy running by, dripping wet after a hard morning of fieldwork. The boy stopped and listened, but he did not turn his head. Your mother whistled again. The boy just stood there, his clipped hair shiny with sweat, and his patched-up clothes bundled him like a cotton sack. Then your mother giggled. The boy turned around, his eyes wide, and then he ran. He ran away. To this day I still did not know if he ran because of your mother's beauty, or because of my bitter melon look."

I chuckled. "You're sweet." Auntie Lau was a good storyteller. She always told me stories I never knew about my mother. Stories I was now dying to know.

"And so are you, Mei," she said. "I suppose you did not know that your mother had a huge fight with your grandfather when she was very young."

I shook my head.

"The next day she disappeared," she continued. "She sent me a letter two months later when she was in Shanghai. A sixteen-year-old peasant girl in Shanghai! I was horrified for her but I dared not tell her father. The next day he came to my father's house and demanded to see me. I was shaking so much that hot tea spilled all over my hand."

"Did he know?"

"Your mother had written him about her reasons to leave. She could not see herself married to a butcher, following her mother's footstep to have seven children. She had stars in her eyes. Mei, I wish she could have seen how much her father cared. He cried. Your grandfather was a good man. He died the day she went on stage for the first time. He never saw her seventeenth birthday."

I looked over at my mother's picture and thought of her as a seventeen-year-old. I never knew my grandfather, and she had never talked about him. It was as if she had buried him with everything else in her past.

"When I came to Hong Kong in 1974, your mother had already made seven films," Auntie Lau said. "Did you ever see her films? Some of them were truly horrific. *Golden Phoenix's Tears*? It made me think of roasted duck soup. But she did make *Morning Rose*, which was a classic. It made her a real star. Have you ever seen it?"

"A million times. On TV when I was a kid."

She laughed. "She loved that film because it reminded her of her father. I believe you heard the rest of the story, how she met your father, and how she became one of the biggest stars in Hong Kong. She was not a bad person, Mei. She had a dream, and she would do anything to get it. And she had a temper. True, true. Were those her flaws? I do not know. But there was a big secret that even the media did not know. You did not know."

She lowered her voice and continued, "She did not quit because she had fights with the studio, about money and some stupid contract. The media got it all wrong. Your father did not force her to quit either." Auntie Lau placed her hand on mine. "She was pregnant with you before she married your father. They had wanted to abort you, but your mother decided to keep you the day they went to Thailand for the procedure.

"Your mother and I kept no secrets from each other," she said calmly and held my gaze. I looked at her, searching for a clue. Then I realized what she meant.

She knew.

"Your mother loved you. She gave up her dream and her life for you." Auntie Lau squeezed my hand and kissed me on the cheek.

I stole a moment with my mother's portrait, then my father's face at the other end of the hall. I didn't see a single tear. Not even my mother's death could make him cry. The last time that stern Chinese man cried was when his only daughter told him she loved a woman.

The marble pedestal gleamed in a corner, its elegance in stark contrast to the licorice-colored, pear-shaped urn sitting on it.

My mother rested in there. It was a wonder how a 130-pound woman could fit into that tiny space. My mother had been five-foot-eight, a tall woman by Chinese standards, and now I could hold her in one hand. Her portrait hung above the urn--she was so young then, her face without a trace of lines, her hair flowing like the Yangzi River. The aunties all said I looked like my mother, save my father's granite nose.

I entered the dining room and set down the bowl of longevity noodles, steaming with plump black mushrooms and a dash of the chili paste my father so loved. I neatly arranged his ivory chopsticks, so used over the years that they had turned tartar yellow, teeming with confused markings where the teeth met the elephant bones.

My father sat alone, by the balcony, resting his head on the glass of the French door, his lanky body arching in a way that reminded me of how, once upon a time, I would crawl into the space between his chest and lap to find my peace. That space didn't exist anymore.

"Baba."

He lifted his head and stared at me in his shadow. He looked pale, and his once-sculpted face was now sunken. Scattered gray locks matched the fog in his eyes. I feared he would slowly drift into that fog and never return.

"Baba, your noodles are ready."

"Rain soon." This was the first time he'd spoken to me in a long time, without my mother's interpretation.

"It's not going to rain. They are going to have fireworks in a few minutes. Do you want to watch?" I helped him up. He didn't resist. We slowly stepped out onto the balcony. The harbor glistened below, thousands of blinking lights of red, gold and green shouting at us. The world beneath us was changing every second my father and I stood in silence.

"Ma loved these bonzais," I finally said, touching the miniature tree next to me. Every fat leaf showed my mother's love for it. Even in her last days she didn't stopped attending to her beloved. The growth in her breasts and her lungs and her bones never stopped her. The trees grew as she shrank.

I crouched down and adjusted the flowerpots, moving the hibiscuses next to the peonies, their blood-red blossoms large and full. Beside my mother's looks, I'd inherited her green thumbs. Gardening had become my new sanctuary, the secret, happy place where life was always happening amidst yesterday's wilts. Birth was not taken for granted. Death was understood. At least the plants never screamed back.

"Your mother loved you," my father suddenly spoke. He waved at me, his trembling voice betraying his calm movement.

"And you?" I dared to ask, not looking forward to the answer.

"I left my father's house when I was fourteen years old," he said. I steadied him as he leaned against the railing and stared at the harbor.

I waited.

"My father owned a farm in Jiangsu," he said. "Acres and acres of fruit trees and vegetables. And horses. Cattle, houses, servants, workers. And two wives. My mother was his second, married into the Li family when she was my age when I left home. But my mothers knew there were many other women. Women with no names. My mother died a sad woman at age twenty-five.

"I hated my father. I would have nothing to do with him and his land and his wealth. I left home with only ten yuen and my school uniform, and I crossed the country in one week and arrived in Guangzhou and stayed with my mother's brother. I eventually crossed over to Hong Kong and worked as a shoemaker for five years, and sent myself to medical school. My sisters and I still kept in touch, but I never wanted to go home. On May 2, 1962, I received a letter from my youngest sister, and she told me my father had been murdered. Shot in the head and his brain splattered in the field, three miles outside of his house. That night I went out and got myself a bottle of brandy and celebrated."

My fingers turned numb. I looked into my father's eyes and they flashed red and green and yellow and purple, as the fireworks started to bloom over the fragrant harbor.

"Why are you telling me this?"

"I am a principled man. Even blood cannot be thicker than principles." He turned to me, his face now bright red, as if he had drunk his brandy. "You asked me if I loved you. I asked my father the same question every day after I left home, even though I thought I hated him. I wanted him to tell me that he loved my mother and he regretted what he did to her. I wanted him to tell me that he loved me more than anything else. But he never did, and I never asked."

"I am asking you now, Baba."

He turned away and stared at the fireworks again.

"Are you still with that..." He couldn't finish the sentence. But I understood.

Yes, I am still with that *woman*, although I didn't know if I should be anymore. But I wasn't going to tell him that. I didn't want to tell him anything, not anymore.

The fireworks died with that resolve. Suddenly, I didn't care if he loved me at all.

He sucked in a breath, exhaled, and spoke again. "I wanted to hate you."

I don't care.

"I wanted to walk away from you and forget about you. It was easy for you to say 'I love that woman,' but it was like you just shot me in the head. Every day I could feel my own brain splattered across that wasted field. Every day I imagined you drinking the brandy at the news of my death. Every day."

The sky started to fall, and the rain slowly licked every inch of our faces and hands. My father stood in front of me, gracefully wiping his face with his hand. His face looked so hard and cold.

"We should eat," he said. I followed him inside and closed the door.

"You were right, Baba," I said.

He turned and studied me.

"About the rain, I mean," I said, as I handed him the porcelain bowl of cold noodles.

At two in the morning, I picked up the phone and dialed. After a couple rings, Jen answered. I was relieved.

"Hi," I whispered.

"Hi," she whispered back.

I sat on the bed and pressed my back against the headboard. The phone line went silent, not even static. I bit my lower lip and held my breath. Then she spoke again.

"You still there?"

"Yeah."

"How did it go?"

"Other than my father hates me? Everything was fine."

"Did you tell him?"

"No."

"Why not?"

"Jen, I don't want to talk about this right now."

"You've got to tell him. He's your father."

There it was again, that condescending tone. I wanted to hang up. I didn't need a sermon on how I should tell my father anything. Not after I'd just cremated my mother. I didn't know why I called in the first place. I hadn't called her for six days. She didn't even ask about my mother, the whole reason for my ten-thousand-mile trip, the whole reason why I was back playing victim to my past.

"I'm so sorry about your mother."

There, she said it. She always had the ability to say the right thing at the very right moment, alleviating every shred of my loathsome feelings for her and reminding me of why I loved her, despite all the doubts about us. The only thing she couldn't do right now was to hold me while I shook and hugged myself, wrapped in my mother's favorite silk blanket.

Jen let me cry.

Eventually I found the box to lock away my emotions in again. "Thank you," I said, wiping tears off my face with the palm of my hand.

"When do you think you're coming home?"

"I don't know." I dropped the phone to my side just as I would drop everything in my life every time she asked me that question. I didn't know. I never did. But it was time to pick everything back up again.

I lifted the phone to my ear.

"...there? Hello?"

"Yeah," I said. "I don't know."

The line went dead for second. "You know, Mei, there really is no hurry."

"I know that," I said.

"I just worry about you. The traveling must have taken a toll on you. The doctor said--"

"I feel fine. My blood pressure is a little high and I tire easily, but I am dealing. I have the meds with me, just in case. You don't have to worry about me. Besides, he needs me."

"But you said--"

"It doesn't matter what I think. What he thinks. He's still my father. That's what we Chinese do."

"What are you going to do there?"

"I don't know."

"Are you going to tell him?"

"Jen."

"I'm sorry, but like you just said, he is your father."

One thing I resented about Jen more than I did her condescension was that she was usually right, and she knew it, and she would not hesitate to tell me either in the context of a forewarning or I-told-you-so deadpan and eye roll.

"I don't know how," I said.

"Simple truth would be a good start."

"Stop it," I said. "The man just lost his wife."

"And he's about to lose his daughter if you don't tell him."

"He won't care."

"Yes, he will. Now, you stop it, Mei. I'm tired of your self-pity and I'm saying this because I love you, even when you treat me like crap. Even when you don't give me half the credit I deserve. But that's not the point. The point is that I love you, and I know your father loves you. And you should tell him. This is important."

I told you so.

For the next few minutes I managed to sidetrack the conversation and avoided the discussion. As usual, we sank into our small talks about the garden and the dogs, how she wanted to repaint the bedroom a more subdued fawn that would match the dirt wall just yards from the tiny window. I couldn't care less. Our lives in New York seemed so remote, the only connection a thin cable linking us under the impossible ocean. All of a sudden, I felt like my soul had aged twenty years, and that life of mine didn't belong to me anymore...

"I love you," she whispered.

"Yeah. Me too." I clicked off.

Auntie Lau greeted me, at On Lueng Teahouse in Wanchai, with a smile so gentle I realized I'd forgotten how it felt to be welcomed. I watched her pour the tea into our tiny cups, her slim, short fingers as frail as bamboo twigs. I was afraid she would break something, break herself. I leaned in to help but she shot me a scolding glance.

Never mess with an elderly Chinese woman and her tea.

"How are you doing, dear?" she said.

"I'm fine."

"There is something you're not telling me," she said. "I can tell."

She winked. She was smarter than she looked, her southern, demure charm a disarming camouflage for her sharp wit. My favorite auntie, although the last time I saw her before this trip was the day I left for the

States and never returned. I had always wished for Auntie Lau to become my mother, and she wasn't even related to me by blood. As I grew up and realized that she would always be Auntie Lau to me, and nothing more, I decided to stop telling her anything as well. I couldn't start now.

"You know too much about me already."

"Do I? But I love secrets. They make me come alive." She laughed. "How is your father?"

"You know him..."

"Your mother's death is very difficult on him."

"He didn't cry."

"You did not cry either."

I played with the half-eaten shrimp dumpling on my plate with my fingers. Suddenly I felt as if I'd regressed thirty years, and now the six-year-old in my head was playing tricks on me. I saw my mother's hand coming at my face, and then heat and pain, and the teacup flew from my little hand, across the room and shattered into pieces, sending the dark liquid everywhere on the hardwood floor.

"...Mei?" Auntie Lau's voice sounded so real.

"Oh, yes, I'm sorry?"

"You went away for a minute. Far, far away."

"I was just thinking about Ma. Did you read those articles about her in the magazines? Absolutely incredible, those people. I'm so glad she's not alive to read that kind of trash."

"Your mother was used to all that. But she was happy to be forgotten for many years even though photographers sometimes still came, when the younger starlets were not available. Your mother was and will always be the most beautiful movie star in the world. She had class. I am surprised they have not noticed you yet. You are so much like her."

"She was beautiful. I have a big nose."

"I mean inside. I can see a lot of your mother in you."

The last thing I wanted to hear was that I was my mother. Every daughter wanted to avoid that fate. I'd tried my best through my young life distancing myself from my mother's world, the midnight reruns of her movies or the thousand-dollar-a-plate charity dinners or the stray snapshots of my pimpled face on the fifth page of *Glitter-World Magazine*. I lived an adult life in the obscurity of suburban New York, paying my taxes and calling out for pizzas and watching cheap rental DVDs. I was nobody's daughter, and I preferred it that way.

"I don't plan on staying here for too long," I said.

She frowned. "But your father—"

"Why does everyone say that? I'm sure he can take care of himself just fine."

"Mei, you are so angry."

I leaned back on my seat and shuddered. Her words sent me off to a place I didn't want to be. Anger. That had always been my elixir and poison, one that had pushed me to accomplish incredible things, then destroyed them as its ample payment. If the other elements of grief were not enough to crush me, anger would simply swallow me until I came out the other end totally changed for the worse. I didn't want that to happen. But angry I was. I could only think of one thing to avert my fate.

I told Auntie Lau everything, then watched her cry and hug me while I felt absolutely numb inside.

I ended up staying with my father for another six days. I sent the maid on vacation and cleaned and scrubbed and made beds and pruned plants and prepared meals, and made myself feel like I was part of this world, this present and future that hadn't existed for me, and would never again. I listened to my father sleep, which he did a lot; most of the time I just wanted to make sure he was still breathing.

On the seventh night I started to pack. Auntie Lau had given me a goose-down coat, such luxury, but it took away half the space in my suitcase. I packed everything else around the jacket, laying them in a circle and filling in every tiny empty space with things I didn't need nor care for. I could have left something, everything, here, but I didn't want to. In a way, I didn't want my father to remember that I'd come back.

After I'd finished, I went to the bathroom to take a shower, and I heard my father in his room, shuffling and moving things and coughing. The man had locked himself in that time capsule and refused to see me except during meals--even he couldn't deny that I made wonderful pork buns, pan-seared noodles, watercress soup and Shanghai dumplings. Food was our only communication; after his long sermon the night of the fireworks we'd stopped talking again.

I don't care.

I kept repeating it so I wouldn't forget.

As I passed his room again, I heard sniffles. I stopped and pressed my ear against the door, the same way I'd tried to listen in on the conversation between him and my mother, many years ago. He spoke in the native dialect that he'd used with my mother. Their secret language; adult talks. Was he talking to my mother's ghost? I shrugged at the notion and decided that I was being unreasonable. The woman was dead. I was nobody's daughter.

Then I heard it.

My father was sobbing.

I hurried back to my room and closed the door behind me, as though I had just seen a woman naked for the first time, an odd mix of shock and exhilaration, blood rushing through my veins and to the top of my skin. As though I'd learned a secret so ripe that I could burst with excitement and shame. Life didn't prepare me for the loneliness that followed, and the yearning that accompanied it.

I stared at my suitcases and knew my world couldn't just fit neatly inside two-by-three hard-shell cases with combination locks. I couldn't just run either. Not anymore.

Gently, I knocked on my father's bedroom door.

"Baba?" He didn't answer. I backed away. Obviously he didn't want to be disturbed. Then I remembered the time Jen and I had fought and I locked myself in the bathroom and refused to talk to her, all the while wishing that she would just barge in and do whatever she wanted to do. Fight. Scream. Accuse me of being unfair. Anything. Instead I got the silence I thought I wanted, and we never recovered from that.

I don't care.

I turned the doorknob and the door clicked open.

"Baba?"

The man sat on the edge of his bed, motionless, with his back to me. He had stopped crying. Instantly I knew what he wanted, as if I'd known my entire life. I was my father's daughter. We were too alike.

I sat on the bed, next to his lanky, slumping body. In his hands he held a black picture frame. He truly missed my mother, I gathered, and the pain must have finally punched him hard enough; it'd reached his heart.

I glanced at the picture, expecting to see my mother's face at her most glorious. Instead, I saw my father and me, a sunny day in May, eighteen years ago. The day I told him about Harvard.

"Baba."

The man lifted his head and looked at me, his eyes deep and dark and fogless. Something was screaming.

I care. I care. I care.

I didn't say anything. The world outside was changing every second my father and I sat in silence. But this time it felt different.

He let out a protracted breath, clenched his jaw, and returned his gaze to the two of us encased in wood and glass. A lot had changed in those eighteen years between the picture and now. And a lot hadn't. The four of us sat motionless in this space, and somehow I felt we were one of the same.

"Mei," my father said, finally. He put the picture down on the bed. "I don't want to hate you."

I had wanted to hear those words for so long, and now that I'd heard them, I revered every single syllable. I remembered, though, what I had wanted Jen to do on the day our relationship turned silent.

I took his hand in mine. He didn't pull away.

"Baba, before I go, I have something to tell you."

He listened.

"Baba..." Simple truth would be a good start. "I'm pregnant, Baba. I'm going to be a mother."

A PLACE BY THE RIVER'S GRACE

(Excerpts from the novel, *Beyond The Banyan Tree*)

Southern Thailand – The Pacific War, March 1943

Tazman could not bunk with the dead boy for another day. He swatted the flies away and picked at the loose skin around the three-inch gash on his left calf. Gangrene would be a terrific way to go. The other men were either sleeping or staring blankly at dark space while they jerked with the freight train's motion. He did not know their names, nor they his; they had met barely two days ago, and he needed no attachments. He leaned against the side of the car, soothed by the joggles, hypnotic clacks and squeals of the wheels on the rails. Through the cracks between the planks, the world outside began to wake: first a shroud as black as giant bats, followed by slivers of light and a diffused dawn.

The sky closed again and poured. Hard.

The men huddled closer to one another to avoid the drips, their odors now stronger than those of the dead peasant and the hay-covered feces in the far corner of the car. Hundreds of miles north of Malaya and Singapore, they still had another day to go until the train arrived in western Thailand. Tazman struggled to stay awake while the others, one after another, drifted to sleep. He reached for the small hatch behind him and slid it open. Rain splattered in, but he stuck his head out and took a few long breaths. The Japanese pigs had bolted shut all the doors, and this small hole was his only connection to the world. Rivers and farms had disappeared with the night, and now there was nothing to see except wall upon wall of the jungle. He then quickly stripped the clothes off the corpse. He grabbed the boy's shoulder and arm, turned the body over and pressed his foot on the shoulder blade, twisting the arm with enough force to pull it out of the socket. He snapped the shoulder by the collarbone and folded the arm around the neck, then the other shoulder and arm. It made no difference to him now whether it was a boy or a rabbit. By the time he was through pushing the body out of the hole, he had worked up a sweat. He picked up a spade and shoveled the feces out as well. For a second, he thought the dead peasant was watching him from the side of the car. He closed his eyes and shook the image from his mind. He had no use for such nonsense.

He rested on the pile of clothes, listened to the rumbling and the rain and the world whisking by through the hole behind him. All he could think of was finding his back to Grace.

Western Thailand – The Pacific War, April 1943

Tazman carried the body for a few hundred yards, slogging through the mire, and soon the grand hole in the ground appeared from the miasma, in the middle of the clearing.

"Carry on," a guard commanded through a megaphone. "Move."

The men reached the edge of the pit. Some of them hunched over and retched. Tazman looked into the mass grave as wide as the Mae Klung River. Bloated, decaying limbs and torsos jutted out from the mounds of muck, amid palls of flies and mosquitoes. A gag rose in his chest, so he steadied himself by leaning on the shovel.

"Are you OK?" one of the white men said, a thick American accent.

Tazman gave him a thumbs-up. The American, his birdcage of a torso the color of fireclay, returned the gesture. He tossed a corpse into the pit, then mumbled a few words and crossed his chest. Tazman dropped his shoulder, and the body he had been carrying tumbled and landed in an obscene position.

"The sooner we get done with this fucking nightmare," the American said, staring at the bodies, "the sooner we can get back to the fucking bridge."

The prisoners had run out of burial ground at the camps and along the railway. The past week, the trucks and bulldozers had done their job burying the remains about a mile from the river. Today, the mudslides had rendered the road impassable for the vehicles, so the men had to carry the bodies for the last quarter-mile. The dead were never buried quickly enough, and soon the prisoners returned to the river outpost and stripped to be hosed down. They clustered against the wall while the hard jets of water assaulted their bodies. It would take hell of a scrubbing to get rid of the stench of death.

"Stand still," the American said.

"When..." Tazman said between mouthfuls of water, "...done with this... nonsense?"

"Not if... Too... Toosey... had any say."

"What?"

"The Japanese... need this bridge... We'll see ... about that."

Tazman pointed at the jet hitting his nether region. "I mean this."
The man laughed and got a mouthful of water. Then he laughed
again. "What's the hurry? This... the best bath I had in months!"

Tazman tried his best to nod and was almost knocked over by the
stream.

They had been working all day, digging holes and nailing stakes and
pouring cement into forms and shoveling gravel and soldering bolts and
erecting beams and lifting rocks. The men mostly kept to themselves, and
Tazman welcomed the solitude while the foremen shouted orders around
him. The blisters on his hands did not hurt much anymore, and by
focusing on the repetition of his tasks, he soon forgot his hunger and
thirst. He hauled two pails of gravel to the left bank of the Mae Khlung,
where the bridge was taking shape within the scaffolding. A few Japanese
engineers surveyed the site while their drones stood guard, but the rest
were mostly shirtless white men busy pouring concrete and raising beams.
These foreign men were the smart ones, the civilized and scientifically
advanced ones. They got to work on the engineering and construction of
the actual bridge. Savages like Tazman could only qualify to dig, shovel,
pound and dive. Shut up and work like a slave. Romusha, or forced
laborers, like him fell like cicada husks, their disappearance seldom
questioned or explained. They might as well never have existed. Tens of
thousands of men had already died on the Burma Railway. White men
had died, too. Tazman could imagine all of them dying alone in a hellish
place thousands of miles from their motherlands, and he certainly did not
wish to call the Mae Khlung River his resting ground. He was determined
to go home. He delivered the gravel, wiped the sweat off his face and
considered the construction again. He had never seen such an
undertaking, the massive structure above him a giant creature with a
gaping mouth. The white men were welding the steel beams and
whistling. He had worked alongside these men for weeks now, but never
had they exchanged a word until today.

Finally the horn sounded. He dragged his body back to the outpost
packed with men ripe with the day's sweat, and began the long march
back to their squalid camp before the night swallowed them.

The following day was no better, the wet heat even more menacing.
Tazman dug and pulled and dragged, and watched one man after another
succumb to the swelter. By midday a few dozen men had fallen ill with
heat exhaustion, but the foremen would give them only moments to
recuperate before sending them off to more tasks. The white men began
to argue, but the flogging came without negotiation. Quietly observing,
Tazman adjusted his taro-leaf hat and took one sip from his canteen. He

could go for days without much food, but he would quickly join the mass grave if he wasted his water. He had learned to pace himself without raising suspicion for indolence, the punishment for which could be death.

Late afternoon, he took a task in the river. The current was strong after the recent storms, but the muddy water was an instant relief from the heat. He was pulling a rope under one of the piers when someone yelped above him. A cable had snapped and the intractable snake thrashed some of the white men. Two lost their balance and fell from the platform into the river. Tazman let go of the rope and swam. Near the bank he found the men, and he pulled them out. One of them, the tall, thin American, had a bone protruding from his arm and was gasping for air. The other was unconscious. Tazman began to resuscitate the second man. A guard approached the bank, shook his rifle and ordered him to step aside, but Tazman continued until the man coughed up water and started breathing. The guard pulled him up by the hair. The American yelled, "Wait a minute..." Yet he could do no more than watch Tazman, who was too exhausted to protest, being dragged away.

The lashing did not last long. Besides, it served to intimidate rather than harm, and neither could daunt Tazman. Then he was sent back to the line, this time breaking rocks by the right bank far from the white men. There would be no further contact between them. The rest of the day passed like a squadron of blood-sucking leeches, and his shoulders and back were as stiff as the fifteen tons of rocks he must have smashed and hauled. The end of the day came as such a relief that he did not mind the long march. Back at the camp, in the shadows between the flickering lamps, the men stripped by the water troughs and washed the grime from their bodies, which were so dark that they could not tell what was dirt and what was skin. Then they dressed and lined up for the evening's rations. The same tasteless shit but a shorter line every day. After he had scoffed down the porridge and cabbage, Tazman crawled back to his space in the wood shed he shared with eleven men. While the others slept, he gazed at the sky through the ceiling cracks. Tonight he so desperately wished to find the lopsided W. His queen in the sky.

Western Thailand – The Pacific War, May 1943

At first it was only a general malaise, and it did not stop Tazman from carrying on with his tasks. They had finished with the concrete piers and steel trusses and begun laying the tracks. He had been looking forward to that accomplishment, even though he realized what the bridge would entail for the Japanese army. He held onto the belief that once they completed the railway, he could go home. Then one night the diarrhea and vomiting came, followed by alternating rigors and fevers that lasted for hours. On the second night, they moved him to the sick ward teeming with diseases and half-corpses. Even as he succumbed to his intermittent delirium, he understood that this could be his last stop.

The nightmares came mostly after the chills. He could not tell reality from dreams while his mind and body burned with pain. The shapeless colors seemed to be eating at his brain, his skin punctured by a thousand pins. And then came the vomiting. He crouched in the corner of the ward, surrounded by faceless shadows, opened his mouth and spewed into a filthy trough. What little was left in him. Bile, blood, stomach acid. Bits of his soul. Then he would slump on his mat, listless, and let the heat consume him. Most of the time he was confused, ready for the end. The dreams grew vigorous during the day. First, they were flashes of the river, jungles, random faces, concocted with the acrid odors of feces, sour cabbage and pus. Then his body felt as if it had turned inside out, his intestines exposed to the sun, his heart outside of his skin, and he could sense every throb bursting through his skull. At times there appeared to be hundreds of flies nesting in his flesh. He tossed and scratched, frantic to get the maggots out from under his skin. The rest of the time he slept, not entirely sure where he was or where he was going. In the few moments between chills and fever, he knew what would happen next. He had seen enough around him: rotting corpses discarded like days-old fish. The life of a war slave. The indignant ending would be fitting for an insignificant life. It was during these lucid moments that he truly believed in his own triviality, his life a statistic.

He was roused by a bright light. Death had come swiftly, and he looked for his mother in the white rays around him. The memory of her consoled him, and he accepted his fate. He let out a sigh of contentment, thinking on how he would see his mother again in the afterlife.

"You're awake."

The American's voice surprised him. Tazman blinked, rubbed his eyes. He tried to get up but the nausea stirred again, so he lay back on the mat and looked up at the stranger.

"Yeah, get some rest," the American said. "You ain't got nowhere else to go anyway."

"What happened?"

"You got sick. Seriously sick. We had to pull you out of that shit hole. You're now at Tamarkan."

"The prison camp for the white men?"

The American laughed. "Yup, and this white man's making sure you stay put here. By the way, I never introduced myself. Captain Andrews." He wanted to reply, but his throat was dry and his tongue tired. "Rest, then," Andrews said. "I'll check on you later."

The sun had already set, and Tazman was chewing on some dried anchovies when Andrews approached the hut. Behind him stood another man, a head shorter but just as scrawny and sure.

"You look much better tonight. Your color has returned," Andrews said. "I want to introduce you officially to Lewis. Sergeant, do you have something to say to the young man?"

Lewis stepped forward and shook Tazman's hand. "The pleasure is mine, sir. And thank you for saving my life." Now Tazman recognized the unconscious man from the river.

"How long have I been out?" Tazman said.

"A couple of days. The Lieutenant-Colonel made sure you got the care you needed. This isn't the Holiday Inn but you can recuperate here. Eat and take your medicine and you should be good as new soon."

"Was it malaria?"

Andrews nodded. "A lot of men have died recently, including some of ours."

"You buried one of them."

"That wasn't our man. His name was Chanarong. Like you, he was a local and a good man. A good friend. We don't want to have to bury another friend."

"But I'm not."

"Yes, indeed you are."

"I mean, I'm not local. Malaya is my home."

Andrews grinned. "Anyway, we were able to get the treatments we needed. I only hope we don't get cholera. That's some nasty shit. Upcountry folks are dropping like flies."

"We had two men from the north," Lewis said. "Many stories of how horrendous everything was at the jungle camps. Cholera, dysentery, gangrene, malaria, you name it. Not to mention they're starving. In fact, we're very lucky here."

"Now, now, don't scare the boy," Andrews said.

"I can deal with the truth."

"Yes you can. Of course you can," Andrews said. "No disrespect, Kai. We're friends here."

"How do you know my name?"

"We know things. And what we don't know, we find out."

Tazman leaned back. "I'm tired."

"You don't trust us, do you?" Andrews regarded him for a few seconds. "I understand you completely. The fact is, you saved both of us. We appreciate that. We've now repaid you for Lewis's life. I still owe you mine. It's not bullshit, it's a promise, but I hope I don't have to repay you anytime soon." He laughed and patted the mat before disappearing with Lewis into the night.

Tazman finished his anchovies and rice, then dropped his tin can and spoon on the ground.

He thought of Grace again. Her smile and hair, and the way she scrunched her nose while scolding him, were more of a concept to him now, and he could no longer afford the luxury of memories. He closed his eyes and listened to the insects and the men around him. The rhythm of chirps, buzzes, inhalations and exhalations calmed him. He started to drift, hoping for a night without dreams or regrets.

Kemasik, Northeastern Malaya – After Liberation, October 1945

The driver yelled again for him to get off the truck. Kai leaped down and stood in the middle of the market square buzzing with the familiar chaos of the scattered stalls, cages, carts, and huts. He had long ago gotten used to the smell of dung and dirt—there were worse things, much worse things—but was surprised by the rich, raw odors of wilted fruit, animal waste and skinned frogs. Such sweet scents of life. Over the severed oxen's heads and blood-soaked feathers, the swarms of flies, a constantly changing mosaic of black specks, were a strangely welcome sight. They were feasting on such a bounty! The senses of the market's dissonance were so overwhelming that he needed a moment to correct his mind.

Yes, this was real.

He knelt, took a handful of mud from the ground and placed his fist under his nose. He took a deep whiff.

Home.

His final memory of Kemasik was that of the throngs of Japanese soldiers instead of flies, the blood of men instead of pigs and squabs, and the clacks of rifles instead of the clangs of cowbells. Yet the scars of war remained visible with the lingering emaciation and weariness, the wandering beggars and the broken doors, the dull eyes and the lethargy outside the square. Behind the promise of an adequate meal, the shadows of war continued to haunt the small town, forever incised in its bones. The young men and women were gone, having been swallowed by the prison camps, conscripted labor, starvation, disease, rape, torture, bullets and bayonets. He did not recognize any of the faces; no one recognized him.

He tightened the knot on the haversack's strap over his shoulder. He limped slightly, his behind sore from the week-long journey in trains and carts and trucks, but he wanted to retrace his steps and reverse the endless march of 1941. This time he had clothes on his body, shoes on his feet, and lunch in his stomach. Everything he would ever need, except for Grace.

The gate astounded him. He had not expected to see it, still intact and erect by the dirt road, every iron rod exactly where it had been, where it should be. The wild weeds in patches along the road to his father's house reminded him of time wasted. The distant fields were awash in verdant green, a sea of grass rippling in the hazy breeze. The trees stood grand and untamed, layers upon layers of foliage and shadows waving at him like old friends. Beyond those emerald crowns and down the narrow brown road lay the fortress of his past.

And then the swell of emotions. He was not prepared for the assault.

He stood in the middle of the driveway. The main house seemed to have shrunk, the pillars discolored or plastered over. The paint on the walls had peeled off in honeycomb patterns, and some of the sculptures had crumbled into chunks and dust. The left side of the house had been boarded up, the walls black as tar underneath the planks. Parts of the front steps had collapsed into pieces. Overgrown with weeds, the driveway was deserted, not even a bicycle or cart. The tourer and motorcycle were long gone. Only dirt and mud puddles welcomed his return.

In the back of the house, the remnants of the camp instantly became a stark mnemonic of misery: listing trestles and barbed wire, scattered bricks, shards of charred wood, fragments of canvas, pile upon pile of rubbish, and over it all, the stench of decay and shit. The grounds were streaked with soot and grease. The sheds that had held him and the other hopeless men leaned like tired ghosts at the periphery. He plodded up the back steps. The door was ajar, and a faint glow emanated from the gloom. He slipped inside, feeling the tightness in his chest as the floorboards creaked under his shoes. The servants' quarters were now vacant and strewn with old trash. The interior smelled of damp mold and wood rot. Thumb-size cockroaches ran freely on the cracked tiled floor and flies hovered everywhere. The stale air squeezed at his nostrils. He passed the storage room and followed the corridor to Juen's bedroom on the right. He peered through the doorway. A candle flickered next to a half-coil of mosquito incense. On the floor, on a wicker mat, lay the shape of a man.

Kai recognized the stumps. "Brother."

Juen did not move.

"Brother," he called again, this time louder.

His brother's arm shifted but slumped back on the mat. He entered the room and pulled up a three-legged stool. Then he sat and watched his brother sleep. Juen's breaths were strong, deep and constant. The stillness pleased him, and he watched his brother sleep for what could have been minutes or hours. When Juen woke and saw Kai's face, he first seemed dazed, as if he could not decide if he were still in his dream. Then came the tethered frown, followed by the widening of eyes, and finally a mouth agape. A mouth that screamed. He pushed himself up and screamed again.

"Shhh... shhh." Kai placed his hand on Juen's shoulder. "It is me."

Kai leaned back against the wall, at once amused and touched by his older brother's hysteria. Eventually Juen settled, and the men stared at each other, not a word exchanged between them. It had been three long years, almost four. Time had hardened his older brother—there were deep new lines on the man's dark, sunken face. Juen had the almost ageless look of the very sick and very old. The spark in his eyes had been replaced by something hard.

Juen held his arms up and seized Kai's shoulders. He gasped, then gasped again. "You are still alive! That night, that night. I thought they shot you and threw you in the river."

"I'm still alive."

"My brother is alive!" Juen yelled as if to tell the world. "You have no idea what this means to me. I can't even describe how I feel." His body shook. "Do you know? Do you know?"

Juen pushed himself up against the wall. Kai had so much to tell his brother, but at the moment there was a whirlwind in his mind and he could not utter another word. Finally he whispered, "What happened here?"

"The locusts left. The Japanese. The men who survived. There is nothing left. They took everything."

"The paintings? The furniture?"

"Everything. Gone. They tried to burn down the house, but Pa stopped them."

"Where is he?" Kai was taken aback by his own question. He had not even thought of the old man for two long years, and now the words tumbled out.

"He went with the committee before I fell asleep."

"What committee?"

"The Communists. They were fighting the Japanese by the end, and now they are in charge."

"Is he a Communist now?"

"No, no. The committee has been questioning him this week. About the war," Juen said. "Pa will be so happy when he sees you."

"It doesn't matter. I didn't come back for him. I want to make sure you're all right. But it doesn't look like you are. This place is filthy. You look like you're starving. You have hardly any clothes."

"We get by."

"Someone needs to take better care of you."

"You, too. You look like shit."

He laughed. "And where are our sisters? How are they?"

His brother did not reply. Instead, his shoulders slumped and his neck retracted, a turtle about to seek refuge in its shell. Then his whole body convulsed in a sob. Kai had never seen him shed one tear, not even on the day he had first seen his own stumps. The proud man had been as stubborn as their father. Now, right before him, Juen had metamorphosed into a figure of grief.

"They are dead, my brother." The truth exploded in Kai's ears. "The Japanese killed them. Our sisters are dead."

He heard the words as clearly as he had seen Juen's tears, but he could not comprehend.

"The bastards," his brother said. "I didn't know, until Pa told me last week. He said the Japanese had..." He swallowed his words and shut his eyes as if trying to erase the horror from his mind.

Kai could not even fathom his sisters' torment. He hoped their end had been swift and merciful. It had been his wish for himself through his days at the prison camps, and he counted himself far too fortunate. He had hoped his brother would be safe under his father's watch, and the girls would return from the factory after the liberation. The memories of his sisters flashed before his eyes. Only now he could not remember their faces and voices. They were only shadows and composites of horror stories he had heard over the years. Then came the sudden guilt: he wished he had known them better, remembered exactly what they had said that last morning. They had made breakfast for their brothers before the men set out for the wild boar hunt. He had promised them a celebratory feast.

They had been thirteen and eleven.

Something clanged on the floor behind him. He turned.

The old man stood at the door, his hair a massive white nest and his once-stocky chest now a wiry birdcage barely hanging on the wide shoulders, his hands shaking and his eyes confused. A tin mug lay sideways on the ground next to a splash of dark liquid.

Juen pushed himself forward. "Pa, Pa. Look, Kai is still alive."

The man's coal eyes did not blink, but he lowered his arms and kept them behind his back. He looked ancient. Extinct. He then cleared his throat. "I made dinner."

"But Pa, it's Kai," Juen said. "He survived, and he came back to us."

"We've all survived," he said. "We don't have much. You can have my portion."

"I'm not hungry," Kai said.

"But I am famished," Juen said.

"You can have mine. Wait here. I will bring it."

Juen pushed himself off the mat. Kai crouched to help him up but his brother waved his hand, then swung his stumps forward and lifted his body off the ground with his arms. "I've learned a few tricks in the last few years."

Their father had made steamed water-spinach with chili paste, such a feast compared to what had been rationed at the camp. There would be no celebratory bird or longevity noodles, however, no pork buns. The men had become accustomed to small portions and bland pulps, enough nutrients to survive another day, and they ate in silent appreciation. The women were all gone, with their female chatter and good will. And men did not talk.

Kai could not remember the last time he had tasted his father's cooking, but he remembered the man's indifference as well as he did the old feasts of pork buns and roasted duck. The Master had balanced his opium habit with a greedy appetite for greasy, rich cuisine. The sweet stench in his mouth had been as nauseating as the lumps of fried intestines and smoked ribs in his paws. The man was now just the skeleton that had hidden inside his old corpulent self. Yet his dual nature, that two-headed snake that threaded through Kai's childhood nightmares, remained the same. He was sure of it.

Juen broke the silence. "What happened to you these last few years?"

"Surviving."

"Yes, but how? We had no idea what they did to you. Where you went."

Kai shot a glance at his father. "You didn't know?"

"No, Pa couldn't get any answers," his brother said.

Kai told them what had happened, about the labor camps in Thailand. He glanced at his father, time to time, the man's expression and tired eyes difficult to decipher. He omitted certain details, but he never embellished. The truth was enough to fascinate his brother, who listened while the spinach turned cold and limp in his bowl. By the time Kai caught up with the present, Juen gripped his younger brother's hand. "It is through our ancestors' grace that you survived all that. How incredible."

"It's certainly a blessing," Wuji said. "But everything is gone now."

"What did the committee want from you, Pa?" Juen said.

The old man gnawed at his food until the leafy stalk disappeared in his maw. He took a sip of water. "Nothing you should be concerned about."

"But the men have come twice already. They seem unhappy with you."

"They're unhappy with everyone. We've gotten rid of the Japanese and replaced them with Communist thugs."

"Pa, don't say that."

"Why? It's the truth."

"People talk."

"Let them hear me. They know how I feel."

"How exactly do you feel?" Kai's voice challenged him.

Wuji glared at him for a second. "About what?"

"Everything. Our sisters' deaths, for instance."

The man's lips quivered slightly. "I did everything I could."

"I don't believe you one bit."

The old man pounded his fists on the table. "Do not speak to me this way. I am your father."

"I'm only speaking my mind. I didn't know what you did or didn't do. I only knew the Japanese spoke to you, a lot, and you got special treatments. Opium, for example."

"I tried to protect you, your brother and sisters. Everyone."

"Then you should have nothing to hide. Not from us. Not from the Communists."

"I don't."

"Brother," Juen interrupted. "What are you doing?"

"I only want the truth. How did she die?"

"How did who die?" Wuji said. "Your sisters? They were raped and tortured by the Japanese. Is that what you want to hear? You want the horrid details?"

"She. How did she die?"

The old man wiped a hand over his face. "You mean your mother? You're still obsessed with her, after all these years?"

"I never got the truth from you."

"What do you want me to say? And I'll say it. That she was a good companion, a good mother, a good woman? That I did all I could to save her life? That I was sorry she died? I was. I still am."

"You're such a liar." He pushed his bowl. It tipped, spinach and rice spilling out. "It was your fault that Ma died. It was your fault that Juen got his legs cut off. It was your fault that we were imprisoned by the Japanese. It was your fault that our sisters died."

"Enough, brother," Juen said.

"He did nothing. He stood and let her die. Let them die. He would have let you die, too. He watched when the Japanese took me away."

"Enough. He's your father. Show some respect."

"He doesn't deserve it."

With that, Kai walked out of the kitchen, walked through the corridor, and walked out of the house he had called home for nineteen years of his life.

He followed the road back to Kemasik and spent the night in a nook between two shacks at the market. The sun had barely crept out when a cascade of soapy water landed on his head. The woman with the bitter-melon face, carrying an empty bucket, yelled at him to leave. He was standing up when she returned with a bamboo stick and shooed him away, but not before he had seized two mangosteens from a shelf and run. In the shade of a camphor tree, he cracked open the shells and devoured the pearly fruit inside. Still hungry, he wandered around the market and looked for pickings. By midmorning he realized that he had no purpose, no more use for the town. And not a cent in his pocket; he had left his haversack at the house. Stupid. The thick spicy aromas of satay and fried sausages showed him no mercy. He decided he could endure one more morning of his father's arrogance and his own impertinence, have a warm meal, gather his belongings, and be well on his way before the sun reached its zenith.

He found his brother in his bedroom, his snores potent and steady. He collected his haversack in the corridor, then rummaged through the shambles in the kitchen and found a few cans of baked beans. He cut a lid open with a carving knife he found in the rubbish, and ate out of the can with his hand. The juice and beans tasted exceptionally sweet this morning, and he emptied a second can. By the third he felt full. He belched and leaned back against the wall, wiped his hands on a rag, and shut his eyes for a moment.

"Were they good?" His brother's voice. "I was afraid you'd left for good."

"I can't leave without saying goodbye."

His brother frowned. "You just got home. Where are you going?"

Kai shrugged.

"He's not a bad man," Juen said. "Why do you hate him so much? He's our father."

"That doesn't mean anything to me."

His brother picked up a can of beans. "This is all we can afford now. Pa sells things, whatever he can find. And there is not much. He'll have to sell the plantation. It's sitting here collecting pests. He's old, and I'm useless."

"Stop. You're not useless. You can do anything you want. You can come with me."

Juen put the can down. "We looked for your body." His voice turned soft, almost a whisper. "He searched up and down the river for days. He pleaded with the Japanese and got a beating. I think you should know that."

Kai gritted his teeth; he would not betray his emotions. "I hope he's good to you. I really do, for your sake."

"You know." Juen looked down at his stumps. "It wasn't his fault."

"I know. It was mine."

His brother's face crinkled, his premature aging evident in every crease. "Don't ever say that again."

Kai wrapped the knife in a rag and shoved it inside his haversack. He had a long journey ahead, and he knew Juen would understand. "I should pay my respects to Ma."

"I'll be right here."

It was all the communication they needed. No matter how old and weary and infirm Juen had become, and no matter how much he still respected and loved their father, he would always be the hero in Kai's story.

For a moment Kai felt lost—he could not find his mother's grave. Had the Japanese destroyed it? He walked along the perimeter and came across a number of graves. He did not know how many men had died here since he had left, but he counted sixteen mounds, fist-sized rocks strewn about at random. There were no other markings, no names, nothing with which to identify the dead. He passed the gravesite, crossed the barbed fence through a jagged tear, and trudged along the dirt path leading to the rubber groves. Suddenly he remembered, and he made a left down an obscure trail and, within minutes, reached the clearing.

There, his mother's tombstone tilted, barely holding on to the mud below. He straightened the stone, pushed his weight into it until it was planted securely in the ground. He ran his fingers over the smooth granite and read every engraved word. Her name and the dates of her birth and death appeared as an echo of the day that seemed a century ago. He shut his eyes and traced the grooves of the etched characters, feeling the hollow under his fingertip.

He listened.

In the breeze the trees whispered around him, sounding like the breaking waves at the beach. She had promised him a life worth living without her. You promised. But he could not blame his mother. She had found her peace. No, she was not the goddess he had worshiped in his youth. Yet in a way, he now felt closer to her. Her remains rested underfoot, but she had been all right, in death and rebirth.

Kai.

He opened his eyes and looked up. The trees beckoned to him, swaying side to side with their kind susurration.

Kai.

Go to the Banyan Spirit, Kai. Go to her.

In this almost alien world of desolation, he yearned for his sanctuary. A place he had always gone when he had felt alone.

He felt alone now.

He found the river, its gentle current and grand rocks old friends waiting for the wayward son's return. He dipped his feet in, the water inviting, almost warm. He had roamed this path a thousand times; he knew every rock and every fork of the stream; he knew how high the water would rise and how low it would recede; he knew how the shadows would swallow everything once the sun sank. Memories were the damnedest thing—they grabbed hold of him and sucked him in. Yet right there and then, as he trudged through the waist-deep water, he became a stranger to this land. His youth seemed to be slipping away with the rolling current, and soon it would vaporize like a drop of moisture in the air, never to return. Because nothing was ever the same. Time changed. People aged. They died. What was left was nothing but yesterday's phantoms.

Once he had crossed, he sat on the bank, his trousers clinging to his legs. The view from this side of the river was breathtaking: the canopy gave hints of the rubber groves, which hugged the distant foothills. The river cut through the jungle, separating civilization from the wilds. In the past he would see the rising plumes from afar, a signal for him to run home for dinner. Now the sky was unmarred except by the specks of black birds and clumps of cumulus gathering above the hills. Rain might come.

He followed the bank upriver until he saw the melon belly of the boulder god, who smiled at him without judgment. He sat by his old friend, took a cut of sugar cane from his haversack and chewed on it, letting the juice seep down his throat and wash away any feelings of guilt and regret. It did not work. He felt more miserable than before, for his solitude now only heightened the reality that he had been a son without a father, a lover without love. Although the shackles and barbed fences and bayonets and rifles had disappeared, a more pervasive prison continued to enslave him. Omnipresent. Psychological. Devastating. The serene vista of river and jungle broke down his last barrier, and he buried his face in his hands. Years of isolation and nightmares finally crushed through the concrete dam in a torrent. He made no attempt to stop; the release of the wound-up tension within surprised him. He heard the Banyan Spirit again. Let it all go. Let go. Let all his sorrow and pain and anger and feeling of impotence go with the river to the open sea after four long years.

He finally got to the top.

The grand banyan stood tall and thick still through the carnage of war, not a scar or broken limb, its aerial roots hanging like curtains of strength. Kai had climbed through its hollow trunk the way he had many times before and crawled out from under its crown again, and he looked into the distance where the curdled sky met the crumpled hills and the crumpled hills met the rolling canopy. The floorboards seethed with spiders and their webs, insects and husks, dust, twigs, and a rumpled bed of bark and leaves, traces of the candles from years ago barely visible. Shadows of that night danced before him.

He planted himself on the edge of the treehouse and dangled his legs far above the ground. He could hear the river through the hoots and croaks of the jungle creatures, though all he could see were trees and patches of the meadow on his left. The world looked so rich and wide and full of possibility. The jungles had always meant certain death for the men entrapped by them. He thought of Sergeant Lewis again, how the man's large hands had held tight as he let out his last breath. And now Lewis was part of this wilderness, his spirit roaming free, free of pain, free of torture, free of the weight of duty and survival.

He took out a stack of paper and a few pencils from his haversack. He searched his mind for words. But words were not enough. He sketched instead. At first, the hatched lines under the tip of his pencil depicted the vast, undulating jungle below the cauliflower clouds, only a hint of the liquid serpent through the fringes. Then there were eyes. All Grace's. Left, right, closed, open, large, small, smiling, frowning, glaring, gazing. He traced every lash and glint from his memory, and the more he drew, the more details he added and the closer he felt to her. He could almost see her now, clacking her heels on the floor planks, snapping her fingers above her face. He had been staring at her, studying her form, counting her eyelashes. At least he had tried, then given up trying and instead fallen drunk with her ballet.

He had promised her, and his promise was true still. He did not know how he would find her, or where, or when. Whether she was still alive. Stop thinking nonsense. She had to be. He had not survived the torment and long journeys only to lose her in the end.

He drew some more. Then he looked up and watched the clouds again, which had grown and flocked closer. Rain would be a welcome relief.

A movement in the meadow attracted his attention. He looked over and expected to see a boar or mongoose looking for prey. Instead, a few men in dark gray clothes hurried through the tall grass, away from the river. Villagers? Hunters, most likely.

Then he thought he saw his father.

He sat upright and looked again. The distance and the dense foliage made it impossible for him to make out the features of the men's faces, but the way one of them staggered and plodded along was confirmation enough.

Curiosity was a dangerous beast, and it had its fat, firm paws on Kai. He left his haversack but took the knife, climbed down the grand banyan and headed toward the meadow. When he got there, the men had disappeared. He studied the ground until he saw their muddy tracks. Three men. One of them unmistakably his father. He followed the tracks to the edge of the jungle. The underbrush thickened and he knew the men could not be far ahead. Then he heard branches snapping, and he stooped and crept forward. The men appeared among the trees. He slipped behind a log and crouched, listened in on their conversation.

"You think we're your personal guards, old man? Taking you back to your house?" a man said. Kai remembered Deng's nasal voice. "You think we're still your servants? Your prisoners?"

"Nobody is anybody's prisoner," Wuji said. "The war is over. We are brothers."

Deng laughed.

"Is that right?" another man said. Kai's back stiffened when he recognized Qing's voice.

"What do you want?" Wuji replied. "The committee has spoken."

"We're not the committee."

"They know nothing," Deng added. "And they were all your dogs in the past. Running dogs. Useless running dogs."

"And how dare you come and bargain with the committee?" Qing said.

"It is not for you to decide," Wuji said.

"We brought you here to seek justice. Our own justice. For what you did and what you deserve."

"What I did? What I did was protect everyone at the camp. Make sure we did the work, so we got treated well."

Kai heard a thud. He rose and peeked above the log. Deng held his fist high in the air. The old man knelt before him, hands tied behind his back. Deng swung his fist and struck Wuji's face.

"You call that being treated well?" Deng said. "Sixteen men died. Sixteen, including my brother."

"What do you want? Money? You already took everything. Everything I owned except for the house itself. You can take it, too. Leave me and my son alone."

"Juen?" Qing sneered. "He's not my concern. He is useless. He won't survive on his own. Not long anyway. And your house? Who wants your ratty old place? Your rubber groves, on the other hand, could be useful to us."

"Take them. Take them all, then. Leave my son and me in peace."

"Look, the old man's giving up so easily. Like he did with the Japanese."

"I already told you I wasn't a collaborator. The committee agreed. They made their judgment."

"The committee knows nothing!" Qing barked. "They weren't there. We were. We watched our families and friends die. We buried them."

"I had nothing to do with it. I was only a liaison. I did my best. My daughters were killed, too."

"Are we supposed to feel sympathy? Besides, we think you had something to do with it."

"You think I helped them kill my daughters? You bastards."

Deng bludgeoned Wuji again.

Kai gritted his teeth. For a long time he had convinced himself that he could not have cared less about his father, but watching him being beaten by these thugs revealed the truth: the old man was still Pa. Juen's

Pa. His Pa. He slipped away from the log and reached a fat oak a few yards away. He started climbing.

"Listen, old man, we don't care about your daughters, or your son," Qing said coldly. "They have paid for your sins, and now you must pay, too."

"Then you are as savage as the Japanese."

"Savage?" Qing raised his voice. "Savage? Look who's preaching? Yes, if it isn't the educated landlord himself, who enjoyed his servants and wives and opium, had his precious children tutored by a red-haired devil, exchanged ideas with the likes of Chiang Kai-Shek, then acted like a cowardly duck, waving his white flag for the glory of the Japanese's reign. You sympathizer. Traitor. Do you know the new dawn now belongs to the Party? We will prevail, and the first step is to do away with maggots like you."

"The committee will know what you did."

"Will they? No one knows we're here. There are so many ways a man like you can disappear. By the time they find your bloated body in the river, no one will recognize you but for your gold teeth. Besides, what if they know? What will they do? Arrest us? We're the future."

"Spare me the propaganda."

Deng raised his fist again, but Qing held it down.

"For the sake of my friendship with your son," Qing said, "I'm offering you your dignity. We won't subject you to the public humiliation you deserve. We'll let you rest in peace in your own backyard."

Wuji spat. "Rubbish. You're doing this here only to protect yourself. So you can get away with murder."

"This is no murder. This is justice."

"Then do it."

"Ah, the gallantry returns. But it's too late. First," Qing said, "I must take a piss."

They laughed. Then they loosened their trousers and urinated on Wuji.

Kai could not dispute part of what they had said, and he did blame his sisters' deaths on the old man. Yet he was not about to watch his father being murdered in their jungle. He had one chance. He grasped the knife's handle and aimed at Deng, who stood closest beneath him. He threw the blade, and it whipped neatly into the man's cheek. Kai leaped down and locked the screaming man in a death grip.

His father had already knocked down Qing, who lay on his back with his trousers down to his ankles. He stamped on the thug's face and swept the pistol toward his son. Kai took it and let go of Deng, who struggled to his feet and pulled the knife from his face, yelping like a hog being slaughtered. Kai swung the gun and struck him the way the thug had struck his father. Only harder. Between his eyes. Deng fell on his back and ceased to move.

"Infants," Wuji said. Then he turned and uttered, "Son."

Kai checked the two men on the ground. "We should go before they gain consciousness."

"Kill them now."

Kai glared at the old man.

"They tried to kill us, remember," his father said.

"No, they tried to kill you."

"And you know they'll kill you and your brother, too."

"Please, don't use Juen and me as your excuse. They wanted only you. There's been enough bloodshed. Enough death. We should go, tell the authorities."

"The committee is the authorities."

"Then we'll tell them the truth."

Wuji laughed. "You heard the bastards. The committee is useless. They'll side with these thugs. The Communists are not to be trusted."

"Still, violence isn't the answer."

"You haven't changed at all. Still full of romantic notions."

"The war didn't break me, if that's what you mean."

The old man's eyes softened. "I'm glad."

An unexpected warmth in his chest confounded Kai, something that had eluded him for much of his young life. The old man did care, seemed genuinely pleased that his son had survived and returned. Then Kai caught a glimpse of his father's arrogant smirk. In a second, the old poison burbled up. Full of romantic notions? The old man could not be more wrong.

"Now, untie me," the old man said.

Kai shoved the pistol in his waist belt.

"Untie me. What are you doing? These thugs will gain consciousness soon. Untie me now."

He approached the old man, who turned around and waited for his release. Instead, Kai grasped the knot and yanked.

Wuji stumbled backward. "What are you doing? I am your father."

Kai could count the veins on the man's forehead and neck. His own face felt hot and swollen. After what he had gone through during the war, he had believed that he had graduated from the pain and rancor, that he had emptied his heart to make room for the British girl alone. But just like that, he was back where he had started, where the pit of unmet expectations had begun to deepen, where his father had declared the broken neck of a rabbit too small to be worthwhile. Years later, the man's disapproval still had its hands firmly around Kai's neck.

Wuji glared at his son. It was not the first time Kai had disobeyed or disrespected him—he had been a wayward child, unlike his older brother—but this time, something felt different. Kai was standing up for himself, and for a brief moment on a narrow strip of grass within the jungle, the two men shared a connection. The moment took Kai back to years ago when he had wrapped his fingers around his father's large, thick hand and wished to grow up stalwart like the grand man before him.

The sky darkened and poured.

"The truth is," Wuji said as if he could hear Kai's thoughts, "I believed you were dead. I made inquiries. They told me nothing. They flogged me. They broke me. Then I heard different versions of the story, that you had been executed, sent to a prison in Singapore, taken to the jungle camps up north. Hundreds of thousands of people had died already. I had no facts. No news. Despite what you think of me, you are my son. I believed I had lost you. And when I heard about your sisters, I wept in my sleep. And not only because of your sisters' fate, but because I knew that when I was gone, your brother would have no one."

"I can take care of him now."

"And I'm grateful to the Buddha that you're still alive. You came back, and our family can be together again."

His father's resigned gratitude seemed genuine. For all of his flaws, the man had never played tricks. A self-absorbed man, yes, but never a sorcerer of words. He realized now that he had loathed his father not for what he was, but for what he was not: warm, loving, comforting, or supportive. He had loathed the old man because of his expectations of what a father should be, much as his father had harbored unrealistic expectations of him.

He picked up the knife and tried to set the old man loose, the downpour making the rope too slick to cut easily.

"Kai!" his father yelled.

Qing struggled to push himself off the ground. Kai patted the pistol on his waist. "Two against one. You lose."

The man's eyes widened. "How did you...? I saw them take you away." His voice was sharp and alarmed. "How did you survive the prison camps?"

"You saw them take me away? How could you know all that?"

The man stood, pulled up and belted his trousers. Kai searched his memories and came to a sudden realization.

"It was you. You lied to the Japanese lieutenant. You set the camp on fire and blamed me. You did all that. It all makes perfect sense now. Qing and his dirty secrets. And you dare to call my father a traitor? You are the traitor."

"Ridiculous. I was a prisoner."

"No, you weren't," Wuji said. "You made a deal with the Japanese and were transferred out of the camp."

Qing charged and knocked Kai on the muddy ground, clasped his hand and shook the knife free. Kai punched him in the face. The cartilage of the man's nose crunched under his fist. Qing let out a loud groan and collapsed on his back.

"Kill him," Wuji said.

He ignored his father and scrambled up. "Tell me something. Is that the only reason you wanted to get rid of me? Because I knew about you and the Japanese soldier?"

The man covered his nose with one hand. "Shut your mouth."

"That you enjoyed each other's company? That you found a way to get out?"

Qing brandished the pistol—he must have pulled it from Kai's belt. He aimed and fired. The bullet whisked past Kai's right ear. Qing fired again. Kai dashed toward the underbrush and hid behind a tree. He heard nothing except the hard rain pelting down. He peered through the downpour but saw nothing. He went down on his belly and moved back toward his father in the mire.

"Come out!" Qing yelled, not too far away.

He slid behind another tree and peered out. In the rain he could barely make out the men's shapes.

"Come out, you coward. Come out!"

Kai glanced up and considered the thick branches above him. Could the same trick work twice? He had no time for another option, so he climbed.

"I know you are still there."

"Run," Wuji said. "Run. Tell the committee what happened here."

Qing stood behind Wuji, who now knelt on the ground, and pointed the gun at the back of his head. Kai crawled on a high branch, inching toward the men below him.

"Incredible," Qing said. "The old man has a spine. How refreshing. You heard your dear father, Kai? Run, like a dog. Run. He is a good man. Yes, indeed, he was."

Qing pulled the trigger.

Kai held onto the branch while his father's body slumped forward and sideways, then coiled until his head flopped and hit the ground with a thump.

His mind went blank.

Then everything turned black.

When he regained consciousness, the sun was setting and the rain had stopped. An intense urge to vomit overwhelmed him, but nothing came. The trees whispered all around him. He looked again, where his father had been, but only shadows taunted him. The conflict of emotions besieged him. The memories of his childhood and his father rushed back, together with the loathing and disgust, then a great sense of loss and confusion. Had it been a dream? Had it happened? He could not tell, and he had not a hint of his exact feelings.

He stumbled back to his father's empty, dark house, the destitution a bleak testimony to the man's fate. A cargo truck was parked in the courtyard, near the back steps at an acute angle—someone had halted the vehicle in a hurry. The muddy tracks were fresh. The engine felt warm. He slipped into the house and followed the corridors until a flickering light ahead stopped him. And voices. Men's voices. Intruders. In Juen's room. He had a thick, sickening knot in his stomach. He imagined his brother's lifeless body, skull cracked open in a pool of blood and brain. He would never forgive himself. Then his brother replied. Kai needed a better view. How many men? What were they doing? He left the house, rounded the corner and felt along the west wall until a light shone through an open window. He leaned close and listened.

"...is true," one man said.

Kai did not recognize the voice, which sounded old, coarse and wobbly. He pressed his face against the lower corner of the window and hid in the shadows. He peeked inside, counted three men about his father's age and in identical dark gray clothes. One of them carried a pistol. In a corner, his brother sat on the floor. His eyes looked tired under the sagging folds of skin, and he jerked as if waking when a man spoke again.

"Did you hear what we said?"

The vacancy on Juen's face quickly turned into puzzlement. Then his nostrils flared. "I don't believe you. My father can't be dead."

"We are sorry. But he is. We'll bring his body to you, and you can see for yourself."

"This doesn't make sense."

"My comrade, the truth is, he killed two men and seriously wounded another," another man said. "We need to know where your brother is."

"I don't know."

"You haven't seen him?"

"No."

"Somehow I don't believe that's true."

"I don't trust you."

"Your father was our friend, our comrade. I've known him for thirty years. I saw you grow up. We would never harm him or your family. But your brother... we all know how he felt about your father."

"You don't know."

"We do. Everyone knows. And Qing told us the same thing. We have witnesses."

"What exactly did he say?"

"Your brother found them in the truck on their way back here. Your father urged him to join the Party, but your brother accused him of being a traitor, for his involvement with the Communists, for causing your sisters' deaths. Your father got angry and they fought. That was when Qing and Deng tried to interfere."

"But he was only one man."

"Your brother is extremely strong and nimble. And he's a good shot. Surely you must know how capable he is, and how he hates your father. Especially what he must have gone through during the war. That and your sisters' deaths."

Kai held his breath when his brother did not answer, holding down the surging grief in his chest.

"We have something else to show you." The man removed a carving knife wrapped in a cloth and presented it to Juen. "Do you recognize this? It's one of the weapons."

"But you said my father was—"

"Yes, yes, he was shot. In the head. But Deng's throat was slit."

Juen let out a low moan.

"But you don't recognize the knife?" the man asked. "This is your brother's knife, and that's Deng's blood on it. Qing was delirious and bleeding profusely when we found him, but we found the knife in Deng's chest. We need to find your brother. We need answers."

"I don't know where he is. And if he did this, he won't come back."

"That may be true. But help us, comrade. Help us find your brother so we can bring this all to order."

"If what you said is true, then he isn't my brother anymore."

"Would you help us bring him to justice, then?"

Juen clenched his jaw. "I'll kill him myself."

The man hesitated. "Well, then, I suppose we will have to find another way. We will leave you in peace now. We are sorry for your father's death." The men nodded before they disappeared out the door.

Kai turned away from the window and pressed his back against the wall, struggling to breathe.

An engine groaned and the truck pulled away. Then there were only the damned cicadas. He peered through the window again. His brother remained still on the floor, but he was holding the blade, the blood there as dark as the expression on his face.

"What have you done?" Juen flung the knife against the opposite wall. "Bastard. Bastard!"

Kai could not listen anymore. He crouched and hugged his knees. And yet his brother's voice boomed in his ears again.

"What have you done?"

Singapore – November 1945

Kai arrived in Singapore in only six days, stealing his way through the villages along the railway. Though liberated, Malaya remained chaotic and impoverished, and no one paid attention to a disheveled man, an obscure man, walking for miles or hitching his rides on the cargo trains and cattle carts. He had nothing except his clothes, but he scraped his way through the bazaars in every town, subsisted on random pickings of fruit and preserved fish. He had no time to mourn. He had made an intransigent decision to bury the past. He needed to start anew as if nothing had happened before; it was the only way he could cope, the only way he could have a future.

After he had crossed the Jorhor Strait, he was struck by a surge of gratitude, and he fell on his knees and kissed the ground. For the first time, he had traveled hundreds of miles on his own terms, through his own free will, with no weapons pointing at his back or the weight of duty crushing him. The custardy mire by the bridge and the shit-brown water were white sand and blue surf through the prism of freedom; his heart almost broke in half as he beheld their beauty.

Singapore was disorienting. Crowded, crooked streets and grand pillared buildings, war-devastated and abused, overloaded his senses: the horns and bells, the constant buzzing of humans and animals, the noise of industry, the half-hearted apologies as shoulders and arms bumped into him, the rich and complex smells of food and rubbish and sewage, and humidity mixed with dust and sand. The burgeoning city, with its post-war paranoia and chaos, still bustled with more life than he could ever fathom. It took him a few hours to navigate, but when he got to the intersection of Smith and Trengganu, it was a homecoming for him, though the corner was as foreign as Coca-Cola or Cream of Wheat. Now, between a Chinese medicine shop and a ramshackle eatery that sold frog leg congee and skinned baby quails, sat the perfectly unhinged door of a place he hoped to call home.

The cramped room on the second floor of the derelict, century-old rowhouse was cluttered with newspapers, paper bags, shredded boxes, and an assortment of China dolls. Kai leaned against the open window and breathed in the thick air perfumed with spicy steam, fish balls, and Chinese herbs.

"Don't sit too close," Dai-Ma said. "There's still broken glass lying around."

She brought him oolong tea and a wedge of sugar cake. Such luxury. He thanked her, then regarded the woman while sipping from the tin cup. His Dai-Ma, his father's first wife, looked frail and haggard for a middle-aged woman. She wore a ratty smock that hid her figure, which he gathered was rather rail-thin. He vaguely remembered her narrow, pointed face, but the long gnarly scar on her left hand was as familiar as the watercolor paintings on her walls.

"It's been a long time, and a whole war. You were only twelve then. How old are you now?" she said.

"Twenty-one."

"Is that right? Time truly is cruel. I'm surprised you remember me."

"I remember your paintings. You used to paint all day, and you would shoo us away."

"I was quite good."

"Was?"

"I don't paint anymore."

He sipped the bitter elixir. Then he practically swallowed the sugar cake, the tea making the mouthful taste extraordinarily sweet.

"How long has it been since your last decent meal?"

He could not answer with his mouth full. He shook his head instead.

"I don't have much else. How about some noodles?"

He did not tell Dai-Ma exactly what had happened at the plantation, nor did she ask. The devastation of war had trained the living to leave the unimaginable to the imagination. The fact that Kai had traveled so far to appear at the door of a woman he had not seen for nine years showed desperation enough.

"How did you find me?" Dai-Ma sat in her chair and watched him slurp up the noodles.

"Juen's mother talked about you from time to time."
She raised an eyebrow. "She did?"
"Then I asked around once I arrived. I was surprised you still live here."
"What if I'd left? What if I'd died? What would you have done?"
"I don't know." He tipped the bowl and quaffed the rest in one gulp, then wiped his mouth with his hand. "I'd think of something else."
"Why me? I haven't been in touch with the family for years."
"You're the only family I've got."
"It can't be true. I was the outcast. What about your mother's brother?"
"He died when I was fifteen."
"I'm sorry. Your father's siblings?"
"It doesn't matter. They are all up north. I needed to come to Singapore. Dai-Ma, can I stay here? At least for a while?"
"This tiny, rundown flat?"
"I promise I won't be any trouble, and I'll pay you rent."
"How do you think you can manage that?"
"There must be something I can do in town."
"Everything is chaotic and difficult after the war."
"People still have to live, they still need things done. Odd jobs."
"What are you good at?"
"Everything." He grinned and extended his hands, palms up. "These can do anything."
"Ah, aren't we a little proud? I don't have much here."
"Dai-Ma, I survived the prison camps."
She narrowed her eyes. When he met her scrutiny with his steadfast gaze, she got up from her chair and began to clear out the stacks of newspapers and boxes near the window. "Well, at the very least you'd love the view."
That evening, he lay on the wicker mat, shirtless with a pair of frayed shorts. The humid air was stale and thick, the racket outside hardly a lullaby. But he had long ago grown accustomed to sleeping through the worst conditions, in the strangest, harshest places. Deep slumber was rare anyhow, his flight instinct fully engaged even after all these years. Yet that was not the reason why he had trouble catching dreams. What kept him up this first night was the urge of finding Grace. The questions ran in circles: What had happened to her? Did she survive the war? Would she remember him? What would he say to her? What would she say to him? He only knew he would honor his own promise to her. He had not survived the war only to go back on his word. He would find her.

He regarded the ceiling blotched with decades of neglect. Then he heard a sigh through the dissonance of street songs. Perhaps he had imagined the British girl. He glanced in the direction of the sigh and saw only shadows.

"Is that you, Dai-Ma?"

A shadow shifted. "I'm only getting something. Go back to sleep."

He lay back on the mat and turned to face the wall, his exhaustion overtaking him. He closed his eyes and listened. He could still feel her presence. In the thick heat, his heart started to warm—no one had watched over him like this since his mother had a long time ago. Then he heard Dai-Ma's soft voice again: "He looks so much like you. So very much."

He opened his eyes. This time, he swore he saw his father's face disappearing into the weaving shadows on the wall.

Within two days he had landed an apprenticeship at the shoemaker's two streets away. His steady hands and concentration had impressed Mr. Nam. Whatever skills Kai lacked were easily compensated for by his endurance, constancy, and dexterity. And he learned fast. Everyone needed shoes. Business would be brisk, and Mr. Nam would be a fool not to employ him and triple his profits. Kai would work fourteen hours a day, seven days a week, with a short break for lunch while Mr. Nam took his midday nap. During that hour, Kai would run to the former British High Commission, the Councils, and everywhere the British might gather—pubs, teahouses, military offices—and ask questions without answers. Every day. The British were in disarray after the liberation, and those who had left were only now trickling back in, but they were his only hope of ever finding Doctor Edward Kendall and his daughter, or an address in distant England, at least a lead. Information. Something. Anything.

He closed the shoe shop and wandered toward Ah-Kee's for two wedges of sugar cake. He was choosing them in his mind when a commotion around the corner drew his attention. Men were yelling, gongs clanking, cans rattling. Street fights were common in the neighborhood, and he wanted to stay out of trouble. He strode toward his Dai-Ma's place. The blast of a siren startled him. A crowd had already gathered near the street corner, under a rope-full of lanterns. Standing by the curb, he watched a small blaze gorge on the woodwork of the third story of a row house, the red-and-white signboard now partially blackened and rickety above the crowd. A fire engine had arrived, and the firefighters urged the onlookers to give way. A few women crouched under an awning, their hands covering their mouths and their faces dark with soot. He was about to leave when one of the women wiped the grime from her face. He leaned against a wall and watched her while the firefighters ushered everyone away from the structure and falling debris. When the women went into an herb shop on the next block, Kai waited a few seconds, then crossed the street and loitered outside. When the women left, he clasped one of them by the arm. She tried to pry his hand away. Instead, he tightened his grip as if he were about to squeeze the life out of her. She uttered a cry and raised her hand to slap him. Then her eyes widened into two pools of shock.

"You!" she trilled.

"Mei, it's been a long time."

"You're still alive."

"So are you. I'm happy to see you, too."

"Oh please, I'm no fool. You never paid me any attention before. I was an insignificant pest in the world of Master Kai Tazman."

"I see you still have that sharp tongue."

A sneer crinkled her face. "What are you doing here? What do you want?"

"Can we talk?"

She regarded him, a hard scrutiny.

"I live only two streets away," he said.

When she did not accept or refuse his invitation, he let go of her arm. She squinted, and then, to his surprise, she slipped her arm into the crook of his and gave it a little nudge.

Back in Dai-Ma's flat, he offered her a chair and a wedge of sugar cake. She glanced around instead, her face twitching. She had aged. The lines around her nose were unforgiving, the smeared mascara and the bags under her eyes almost sinister in the dim room.

"What is this crummy place? Master Kai doesn't really live here, does he?" she said. "And stop staring at me."

"It's been a long time. I still can't believe it."

"How long have you been living here? What are you doing with all the China dolls?"

"I torture them."

She winced and cleared her throat. "Some things never change."

"A lot hasn't changed. That's right. Like you."

Her face twitched again, but she settled a hard gaze on him.

"Tell me about you," he said. "You live in that building, the one that was burning?"

"Have you been stalking me?"

"Now, why would I do that?"

"You tell me."

He grinned. "I only just saw you on the street. It was a coincidence. I swear."

"Oh," she uttered. He could have been mistaken, but she sounded disappointed. "What do you want from me, then?"

"You're only the second person I know here. Is it wrong to need people?"

Her laugh was shrill. He remembered it like the cold hard jet of water at the prison camps. Mei was not unattractive. In fact, to many men, she could be described as agreeable, with all the appropriate, proportional features, of which even his mother would have approved. With better mascara, a subtler shade of lipstick and cosmetics to hide the lines and bags under the eyes, she could pass as desirable. Her cold laugh, however, exposed her as anything but. Lost in these thoughts, he could not keep his eyes off her.

She shifted in the chair. "You haven't answered me. How long have you been living here?"

"A few weeks. This is my Dai-Ma's flat."

"Your Dai-Ma?"

"My father's first wife. She left before you came to work for us."

"Why did she?"

"As far as I know, she couldn't bear children, so my father kicked her out."

"That doesn't surprise me." She shifted again. "And your brother?"

He looked out the window. No past, only the future. And certainly he was not about to tell her more than she should know. "They're all fine up north. But it doesn't matter now. I want to start anew here."

"Here? In this?"

"It's a start. It doesn't seem that you're doing any better than I am, judging from that building you live in."

She laughed again, but this time gentler and more resigned. "It looks like we do have something in common."

He considered her remark and nodded. "Are you sure you don't want anything to eat?"

"Noodles," she said. "I'm starving for some curried noodles."

The British continued to trickle in, a ship here and a train there, and they began to set up shops and rebuild their establishments. Kai visited as many as possible, asking questions, often met with blank looks or indifferent shrugs. He had written letters and inquiries but received no responses. He worked hard and saved his wages. He had had dim sum with Mei some afternoons at a teahouse about five blocks from Trengganu. They met again one evening for a late snack after he had closed the shop. Her awful laugh still bothered him, but her familiarity was comforting. He had wanted to forget his past, but his new friendship with his former servant sparked an exciting prospect. He had never had a relationship with a woman other than his mother (Grace had been only fifteen, after all), and this felt different. For one thing, Mei and he spoke the same language, laughed at the same cultural absurdities. No books or homework or childish bickering. Instead, there was something else. Despite his distaste for her, he also found her appealing. She did know how to make herself presentable with cosmetics, her blemishes no longer detectable, her feminine features accentuated. Now he often caught himself staring not at her face, but at her breasts rising and falling beneath her dress. Like now. His eyes met hers, which suggested something more primal than conversation. He looked away, his ears burning, and felt her hand on his.

"It's chilly here," she said.

"What? It's thirty-two degrees."

"Can we go somewhere else? Your flat? Is your Dai-Ma home?"

"She's still at the doll factory, I believe."

"Shall we, then?"

"But I thought you hated that crummy place."

"I do." She laughed. "But I'm tired of sitting here."

"I like the barbecue pork."

"Shall we?"

He caught the curl of her lips, almost challenging with disdain. Something pulled at him. The bright red, perhaps. He nodded.

It was the first time she had entered the small flat since the night of the fire, and the disapproving moue on her face returned. She pushed away the books and sat on the wicker mat. "These books weren't here last time. Do you read?"

Suddenly he was unable to speak. In the pale light, the way she sat on the mat, one hand on her hip and the other gently rubbing her neck, put sinful thoughts in his mind. She patted the space beside her. Like sorcery, her beckoning compelled him to obey, so he sat next to her. Close. She had a deep and rich scent, like the thickest of rose bouquets or a ginger garden. Maybe paprika. He could not tell. Instead, he concerned himself with the tightness in his groin and the heat of his face when she took his hand and placed it on her chest.

"You smell nice," he said.

"I should. It's expensive."

"What is?"

"Oh, silly man." Her eyes widened. "Have you ever? You've never, have you?"

"What?"

She took his other hand and placed it on her thigh. "This."

She leaned forward and pressed her lips on his. They were waxy, bitter like tea, but just as warm. His erection became uncomfortable against his trousers, so he shifted his weight, lost his balance and fell forward. Now his chest was pressing on hers, his hands sandwiched in between, and her nipples nudged through the thin fabric. She kissed him again, this time her tongue invading his mouth. The sensation set him quivering, and she wrapped her arms around his neck and pulled him toward her. Soon he could not tell hands from hands or mouth from mouth.

Nothing made sense anymore.

He had dreamt about this. Vivid fantasies, even in the pit of the jungle and the depth of his misery. It was one of the few things that had sustained him.

No. Not this.

He opened his eyes and watched her face turn into a mosaic he could not recognize.

No. Not this at all.

He pushed her away. She grasped him again, but he forced himself up and pulled up his trousers.

"What are you doing?" she said.

"You should leave."

"You must be joking."

"I'll walk you home."

She clenched her jaw and glared at him. That menace again. She buttoned up her blouse with rapid fingers and, before he could utter another word, dashed out of the flat.

A young woman's pride is even easier to bruise than a man's. After Mei had not visited him for two weeks, Kai decided to look for her. He closed the shoe shop at exactly ten o'clock and picked out some sunflowers at the market. Holding the bouquet and standing among the gutted fish and plucked chickens, he chuckled to himself: *What am I doing?* The confusion was unlike anything he had experienced before. He could still smell her, and he would be a hypocrite to deny that he had thought about her in the past two weeks. He had. Of her lips, her breasts, the erect nipples. Of all the sins he had wanted to commit with her. Thinking of them now made him hard. And yet there was another side of him that pulled him away. The side that had endured the pain and horror of the war. The side that had watched his father die and heard his brother's cry of betrayal. The side that had made a promise to Grace.

By the time he reached the building, he had serious doubts about why he was there. Nonetheless, he gripped the flowers and walked through the open passageway. He had expected a typical courtyard or lobby, stairwells and cracked tile floors, a dog or two, lines of garments hanging out to dry, naked infants in their washbasins, old men and women squatting on their three-legged stools and picking at the crusty scabs on their arms and faces. Instead, he came through an obscure door and entered a long, narrow, dimly-lit hall filled with men and smoke. There was a bar on the right with many bottles of liquor. The men sat and stood around small tables, many smoking cigarettes and drinking from their glasses or cups. The sunflowers in his hand looked ridiculous now, and he hid them behind his back. A woman in a gaudy red dress approached him, her face ghoulish, painted on. She looked to be about Dai-Ma's age. There was suspicion in her eyes, and her crooked smile seemed disingenuous. Her eager generosity to offer him a chair and her gentle tugging of his arm appeared to be more theatrical than real. But what did he know? He was no expert on the opposite sex.

"Welcome, mister." She pulled a table toward them. "Welcome, welcome, welcome. I've never seen you here before, ay?"

"I'm here looking for someone."

"Aren't we all, ay? You want something to drink? Or eat?"

"I'm very hungry."

"What are you in the mood for, mister? How about some scallion pancakes and pot-stickers?" Then she thought of something. "You have money?"

"Of course." He pulled a few notes from his pocket.

"Oh, don't be offended, mister. But you look so young and... anyway, wait here and Lan Fa will take good care of you."

She left without giving him a chance to reply. He was fine with her suggestions, though. He was famished. He set the flowers on the table and looked around. The men acted jovial, if rough, loud, and callous. A multitude of waitresses shuttled among the clusters of tables, often sitting with their patrons, at times in close proximity. There were two white men, in their sailor uniforms, chatting with their lady friend in a corner. Kai became curious about them. Their conversation looked animated, and the men kept stroking their friend's naked arms. *Foreigners don't have much modesty, do they?* He thought of Andrews and smiled. *No, they don't.*

He had not imagined Mei living above a restaurant, and he wondered if she worked here as well, and why she had never invited him over for supper. Perhaps she was embarrassed, but unnecessarily so—he was only a shoemaker's apprentice. He straightened his white tee-shirt and realized that he must look like a coolie. No wonder Lan Fa had looked suspicious. He should have gone home and changed into his nice shirt and trousers. He was about to leave when Lan Fa returned with a short porcelain bottle and two tiny cups.

"Have some rice wine," she said.

"No, thank you."

"It's on the house. No charge, no charge."

"I don't drink."

She laughed. "A little wine won't hurt you." She poured the wine into the cups and handed him one. "*Gan bei.*" She sat, tilted her head and swallowed every drop of her wine. "*Gan bei. Gan bei.* Go on."

He emptied the cup. The liquor burned his throat and hollowed out his chest. He choked and coughed, the bitterness instantly turning into an intense heat on his face and neck, followed by pressure on his temples, as if two large vices had clamped the sides his head. He coughed again, and Lan Fa laughed encouragingly. In another second, the warmth spread through his arms and body, the soreness in his shoulders melted away. He rested his arms on the table, letting the sensation wash over him, and the hall brightened in an instant. Now, Lan Fa's eyelids opened and shut like two giant clams, and her lips quavered when she laughed, two rows of yellow teeth gleaming. She was the ugliest woman he had ever met.

He reached for the bottle, and she pressed a hand on his. "Ay, ay, slow down."

"I feel fine."

"I know you do, and I'm happy you do. But this liquor is strong. You need to take it slow."

"Why?"

She brushed her fingers over the hair on his arm. "Don't you like Lan Fa?"

"I do," he lied. The heat in his groin was betraying him.

"You want to take me upstairs, then?"

"Huh?"

"I told you Lan Fa will take care of you."

"I appreciate it. But I'm here to find a woman."

"What am I, then?" She grinned. "Am I not woman enough for you?"

"I mean I'm here for Mei."

Her smile disappeared. "Mei?"

"Yes, Mei. Do you know her?"

"Everybody wants Mei. Every damned bast-- She is a lovely girl." She looked down at the table and noticed the sunflowers there. She frowned, then smiled a crooked, nasty smile. "Clearly I have wasted your time."

She got up and sauntered past the bar toward the back of the hall. Kai reached for the last of the rice wine. The potent liquid sent another wave of heat through his body. His fingers and toes curled and the tip of his tongue went numb. He noticed something new about the men and women, especially the latter. Their ornate faces, their slithering mannerisms, their rippling laughter. Salacious. This was no ordinary restaurant. He had an erection, so he sat upright and crossed his legs. He started to laugh.

This was absurd. What would Grace say about this. Barbaric!

His heart went sour for a moment. *Barbaric!* He could hear her voice so clearly. She was sitting right next to him now, scowling at him, scolding him.

You backward chauvinist.

The sailors in the corner stood. One of them took the woman's arm and yanked her to him. Both men laughed, then the other one jerked her toward him, and she bounced from man to man, a bone between two dogs. One man grasped her behind and pulled her close. The other man licked the sweat and liquor off his upper lip, then leaned in and pressed his nose against her nape. She swung her head toward him and whispered, and he tapped his shipmate on the shoulder. They both grinned as if they had found gold.

Kai approached the sailors ascending the stairs. He could smell the alcohol on his own breath, and he cleared his throat and hollered in his best British accent. "Pardon me, sirs."

It came out sounding like a mockery. The men turned and regarded him, then turned back to climb the stairs.

"Pardon me, sirs."

"Bugger off," one of them said.

"I have a question for you, sirs."

"Hey boy, I said bugger off."

"I don't mean to intrude, but I have a question for you."

"What makes you think I know the answer to your bloody question?"

"Because you're British."

It seemed to pique their interest. The men turned and regarded him again, this time with amusement in their eyes. "What do you want, boy?" the one with the blue eyes said.

"I'm wondering, sirs, if you know the whereabouts of a Doctor Edward Kendall."

"Who?"

"Doctor Edward Kendall."

"No. Now, bugger off."

"Are you sure?"

"I said no. Check the hospitals or clinics."

"You don't have to be so fucking rude."

"What did you say?"

"I said..." He had a bitter taste on the tip of the tongue. Words would not come, so he turned to leave.

"What an asshole," the man said behind him.

Heat swelled in his head, and he staggered toward the table. Normally he would not tolerate an insult from an *orang asing*, but the warmth in his fingers and toes gave him such pleasure. He felt a hand on his shoulder and turned to see a red-faced sailor. He clenched and raised his fist. He had not wanted a fight, but if it had come to that, he was no slouch. He would crush that straight, perfect nose. He knew just where to land the punch.

"Did you say 'Kendall'?" the man asked.

He relaxed his fist. "Yes. Doctor Edward Kendall."

"I've heard that name before."

"Yes? Where?"

"The correct question is when. It was a few years ago. I was at St. Andrews, at the service."

"Service?"

"Yes, memorial service. I clearly remember they mentioned the name of a Doctor Edward Kendall who died on the *Prince of Wales*. Because my brother's name's Edward, too."

"What did you say?"

"The *Prince of Wales*. Certainly you've heard of it, and the ghastly attacks? Tenth of December, Nineteen Forty-One."

"Did you say he died?"

"That's exactly what I said. We had a damn service. All the officers were there. It was a somber affair."

"What about his daughter? Do you know where she was?"

The sailor shook his head. "I'm sorry, mate. Nothing. The doctor's name barely registered with me. I wish I could be of help, but you see, I have an appointment with destiny right now." He smirked. "Good luck, boy."

Kai slumped in his chair and watched the sailor return to his companions on the staircase. Part of him was deflated by the news, but part of him decided to refuse it, deny it, for he could not believe that this had been the doctor's fate. And if the sailor was telling the truth, Grace could be anywhere. She could have died already. The revelation sent a chill through him, dispelling the warmth in his body. He glanced at the bouquet, its brightness now nauseating. The noises around him rushed in, amplified and obnoxious, attacking his senses, and the muted shapes of the room spun around him. He steadied his hand on the table, felt feverish again, but no longer with tingly pleasure. The garish flowers wavered and expanded and swirled and pulsated.

That was the last thing he remembered before he opened his eyes to see Mei's carefully painted-on face.

"Ay, wake up."

He murmured, but had no idea what he said.

"Wake up," she said. "You blacked out."

"I what?"

"You had too much to drink. Overestimated yourself again, didn't you? Ay, ay, you are going to vomit."

He suppressed the urge and blocked out the light with a hand.

"Why are you here?" she said.

"I was looking for you. I wanted to apologize for what happened the other night."

"Oh please," she sneered. "You were very clear about what you didn't want."

"What's this place anyway?"

"You don't know?" She looked surprised, then laughed. "You really don't know? You're so naive. You've never been to a brothel before?"

"You live above a brothel?"

"I work here." She raised her voice. "So now you know. Not that it makes any difference."

He leaned in and pushed the sunflowers toward her. "I brought you these."

She touched the flowers, her face softening for a second before she snapped her hand away. "Ten-cent flowers from the fish market. You're really classy, Tazman. Now that you've delivered the flowers, you can leave." She stood and started toward the bar.

"Wait."

"What?"

"So, you and those sailors..."

Her snicker had an edge that sliced the air. "Yes, sailors, shopkeepers, officers, bricklayers. Your insult won't hurt me."

"I'm not insulting you. I don't really care what you do."

"Precisely." She turned and walked away.

He staggered up and grasped her arm. She swung and tried to shake him off. He pulled her toward him, his strength overpowering her. "I like you, Mei."

"You're such a liar."

He stiffened his shoulders. "Don't call me a liar."

"What do you want from me?"

"I need your help."

"And why should I help you?"

"Because we're friends."

That shrill, cold laugh again. "We are? Because I worked for your father for a few years? Because we had tea a few times? Because I let you touch my breasts?"

"Because you like me."

"Kai Tazman. Really?" She did not wait for his reply but quickened her pace toward the bar. He leapt forward and clasped her hand again.

"Let go," she barked.

"Those sailors, the British men. I need to ask for their help. When you see them—"

"When did I become your confidant? Your messenger?"

"Please. Do this for me? And I'll make it up to you."

She narrowed her eyes.

"Please, I beg of you," he said.

"It must be very important."

"It is. I know you don't trust me, but a promise is a promise. As long as you get me what I want to know, I'll make it worthwhile for you."

She scrutinized him, her eyes two dark slits. Then her lips twisted into a smile. "Now we're talking business. What do you need?"

"I need to find Grace Kendall."

Her smile disappeared.

"Do you remember the doctor's daughter?" he said.

"Oh, the precious white girl." The expression on her face had not changed the slightest, her voice flat as the low hum of the fans. "I haven't seen her for years. She's probably back in her country. What do you want from her?"

"I have questions. I know about the doctor, her father. But nothing else."

"What about him?"

"He died."

"And you don't think she's dead as well?"

He gritted his teeth. "She can't be."

"Why can't she be? We had a long, horrible war."

"She can't be. I just know."

"Please, aren't you romantic?"

"Will you or will you not help me?"

She regarded him again for a moment. "Of course. As long as you'll make it worthwhile for me."

He handed her the flowers.

"I'll see what I can do," she said. "What I can find out from these British men."

He leaned in and kissed her on the cheek.

"What was that for?" Her wide eyes suggested genuine surprise.

"A promise is a promise. You have my word." All afternoon he could not concentrate, his hands trembling, losing their usual dexterity. Mr. Nam scolded him for the unsightly seams and uneven stitches, demanded that he do them over, snapped that young men like Kai no longer showed any pride in hard work for an honest living. Then Mr. Nam needed to rest, and deferred his own queue of work orders to the ungrateful young man. Once the shoemaker had retreated to the back room, Kai pulled the note from his pocket and read it again:

Meet me at the Celestial Palace at 10 tonight... I have important information... Ask Madam Chin for me... Mei

Her scribbling might as well be sprinkled with gold and diamonds. For the first time in four years, he might have a lead on Grace's whereabouts, and the fact that Mei had not delivered bad news meant there was hope. He focused on clearing his workbench before ten o'clock.

He arrived shortly after ten and asked for Madam Chin. This time he noticed the smells and sounds of his surroundings: fish cakes, fried turnips, soy chicken, alcohol, cigarettes and perfume; chatter, laughter, quarrels, teases, flirtations, refusals. Every table and chair had its purpose in its seemingly random placement, first and foremost to keep the men from leaving. In fact, the drinking hall, the constant shuttling in of women in revealing dresses, and the auspicious staircase that ascended and disappeared behind a fall of red beads reminded him of a trap. The jovial, unsuspecting men were nothing but hapless prey, and the women the bait. Kai was not sure who the hunters were.

So this was what a whorehouse looked like. It all made sense to him now, the way Mei dressed and acted, the way she had seduced him. He felt guilty and gullible for falling into her trap, but he was not entirely innocent or regretful. The sensations of being close to a woman, smelling her, touching her, tasting her, only deepened his desire to find Grace.

Moments later, an older woman, perhaps in her sixties, approached him with hard eyes. Certainly no woman of interest—at least Lan Fa had a bountiful chest and a full set of teeth—yet that had not stopped her from painting her face with as many colors as the others. When she smiled, her breath was a cocktail of cigarettes and pickled cabbage. "You must be Master Kai. Mei told me all about you. What a handsome young man you are."

"Where is she?"

"She's waiting for you upstairs."

"Upstairs? Can you ask her to come down?"

"Master Kai, you must know, this is a place of business, not for private conversations and friendly gatherings."

"I'll pay for the food and tea."

She grinned and tugged at his arm. "She's waiting upstairs. You'll have all the privacy you need."

He wondered why they needed privacy. Then a dreadful feeling sank in: What if Mei did have bad news? To prevent him from making a public spectacle of himself? With trepidation, he pushed through the beaded curtains and entered what looked to be a dim maze of plastered walls and draped doors. Madam Chin led him through the hallway thick with perfume, cigarette smoke and sweat. Kai could not deny the sexual vibrancy of the place, and he got a glimpse here and a peek there of skin, silk, acts of lust. He was, of course, no sheltered pup; he knew well what sex was about. Yet he had never been with a woman. It was an indisputable fact, his secret, which he did not feel an urgent need to profess or deny. He had to focus on what he had come for. Madam Chin stopped at a hanging flower-print sheet, turned and squinted at him. No need for introduction or explanation. Kai pushed the sheet aside and entered.

Mei greeted him with a cocked eyebrow. She sat in a chair at the wall, smoking a cigarette in a long filter. What surprised him was the presence of another young woman in the cramped room, whose tired face was unfamiliar to him. For a second he felt his deflation: he had hoped to see the *asing* girl there.

Mei stubbed out the cigarette in an ashtray and stood. "Master Kai Tazman! I'm so glad you can come tonight. I've been expecting you, Mr. Tazman." Her tone was uncharacteristically formal and cordial. Then she clutched and patted the young woman's hand. "Thank you so much,

Violet. But now, I have an appointment with Master Kai Tazman. Could you wait another half hour and we can finish our chat?"

Violet stole a glance at him before leaving them alone.

"Please sit." The chill in Mei's voice returned.

"Why did you say we had an appointment? You made it sound like..."

"Relax. No one cares. Besides, Violet is a sister. Please sit." She offered him the chair and sat on the bed. "Why do you feel so uncomfortable? Don't you like this place? There are women everywhere."

He sat, but did not answer her.

"You think this is disgusting, do you? What I do is disgusting?"

"I already said I don't care what you do."

"I can tell. Your eyes reveal your feelings."

He shifted in his chair. "You said you had information."

"I got what you asked for, yes."

"And?"

"She's still alive, and she's in Singapore."

He sat upright. She could have easily told him everything in the note. "What are you not telling me?"

She pressed her lips together. "You don't trust me? Then why did you even ask me?"

"Where is she now?"

"Before I tell you anything, there's something I need from you."

"What is it?"

"You promised me you'd make this worth my while."

"I will."

"I want you to pay first."

"And why would I do that?"

"Do you want the information or not?"

"It's blackmail."

"No, it's not. It's called bargaining. I'm not willing to give up the goods without payment first."

He considered her words. "I don't have much money. You know that."

She lay on the bed and patted the space beside her.

"I already made it clear," he said.

That shrill laugh again. "Please, I'm not going to eat you up, if that's what you're afraid of. So, what's the harm of keeping me company for a little while?"

"What do you really want from me?"

Her face turned solemn. "Rest with me for a while. Hold me."

"That's all?"

"I don't want anything else from you. I know I can't, so I won't even ask. But I'm lonely. Surely you can understand loneliness."

He realized that he was nodding his head. He stopped himself.

"I could use some compassion," she said. "You told me we're friends. Can't a friend keep another friend company? Is it too much to ask?"

The sincerity in her voice surprised him, and she had spoken the truth. She was a link to his past and a glimpse of what the future might bring, proof that two people so different could find each other in a strange, twisted city, following a thread of desire. Desire to connect. He slid onto the bed. She lay sideways and faced the wall, then reached back, grasped his hand and pulled it toward her. He rested beside her, let her pull his arm around her shoulder. Her body felt small in his embrace. The fragrance on her neck was foreign, arousing, like nectar luring a bee into a blossom's core. He pressed his chin there and drank in her scent. She was the *asing* girl.

He visited the barbershop and purchased a pair of well-polished wingtip shoes. After Dai-Ma had left for the factory, he put on his best shirt and slacks, pressed to crisp sophistication. He folded two ten-dollar bills, an advance he had wrestled out of Mr. Nam, in his new leather wallet. He even bought a gray fedora that reminded him of Humphrey Bogart. He followed Mei's instructions and strode through the maze of narrow streets and past the bazaar by the river. What the people had done in this neighborhood, so soon after the war, was remarkable. The strings of lights and bright signs dazzled him, momentarily wiping away the post-war devastation that had continued to eat at the city's soul. Here, in the glitter of neon and the aromas of vendor-lined sidewalks, he came to luxuriate in his own Casablanca. With a swagger, he entered a row house, convinced that he was Blaine looking for his Ilsa.

He had expected an atrium or grand foyer. Instead, he climbed a tall staircase to reach an empty room. Stains dappled the walls and floors, an odor of bleach pervasive, as if the place had only recently been cleared out and was in the middle of a renovation. He tapped on the bell, its brittle chime echoing between the walls. A few seconds later, a side door creaked open and a young woman entered. She introduced herself as Peony and apologized for the room's condition. She asked if he had an appointment. He lied, then asked for Bugloss. It was a strange name, but Mei had insisted that he ask for Bugloss and no one else.

Peony frowned. "Bugloss?"

"Yes, Bugloss. I'm here to see Bugloss."

"How do you... She isn't here today. I'm very sorry. You may come back tomorrow."

She asked for his name, and for some strange reason he said, "Nam."

When he left, he bumped into a balding man who wore a cheap, ill-fitting suit. The man tipped his hat, and Kai did the same. Halfway down the stairs he heard the desk bell dinging.

The next day, he showed up at the same hour, wearing the same clothes and hat as the day before. He approached the desk and clinked the bell. After a brief moment, the door creaked open and a young woman appeared.

"Miss Violet? You work here?"

"Yes, yes, of course. Mr. Tazman, may I help you?"

"I'm here to see Bugloss. I have an appointment. And I have money."

Violet regarded him for a brief moment, then asked him to follow her through the door, down a narrow corridor into a small waiting room. She shut the bamboo doors on her way out. A hint of lilac softened the sparsely decorated room, blank walls touched by the weak light of a floral lamp that rested on an end table, next to two wooden chairs. He listened to the hushed voices of women in the corridor and waited, unsettled by a feeling in his guts that he could not fathom. Then he remembered what Mei had said about the girl.

"Violet is a sister."

He pushed open the doors and peered out. At the end of the

hallway, two women were whispering. One of them looked like Peony from the day before, and the other... Could she be? Was that Grace? When they saw him, the chatter stopped and they stepped away. He followed them, but a voice called behind him.

"Mr. Nam."

A short but muscular man stood outside the waiting room and waved him over. "Mr. Nam," the man said. "I'm sorry, but Bugloss can't see you today."

"I have an appointment."

"I'm very sorry."

"Should I come back tomorrow?"

"I'm sorry. I can't tell you. But now, would you please leave?"

"Why?" He reached inside his pocket and pulled out his wallet. "I have money."

"Please, Mr. Nam. I've been asked to escort you out of the building."

"Why? What did I do?"

"Please, Mr. Nam." The man lifted his shirt to reveal a holstered revolver. "I will not ask you again."

Kai burst into Mei's room. She screamed and seized the robe hanging on the chair by her bed. The naked man above her did not stop, so she pushed him away. He was short and thin and landed awkwardly, half on the bed, half on the floor.

"Get out," she yelled. "Get out, now."

Kai glared, pointed his finger at Mei as he left the room. A moment later, the other man, now fully dressed, rushed out of the room and spat at him before stomping down the stairs.

"What in the hell?" Mei barked as she peered out, wrapped in her red robe.

"Did I interrupt something?" he sneered.

She grabbed him by the shoulder and pulled him into the room. "How did you get up here?"

"I paid. Handsomely."

"What do you want?"

"What is that place you sent me?"

She scrutinized him for a moment, seemingly unsure what he had meant. Then she laughed. "You know what it is."

"What kind of game are you playing?"

"Game? You asked me for information and I told you exactly what you wanted to know."

"I asked you about Grace. Why did you send me there? Who is this Bugloss person?"

She lit a cigarette and took a deep draw. "Bugloss is Grace."

He clenched his jaw and seized her arm. "You're lying."

"Let go of me, you ass."

"Not until you tell me the truth."

"I am. The truth is harsh, isn't it? Your precious little white girl is a prostitute."

"Stop lying!" He squeezed his hands around her arms, feeling the veins in his forehead pulsating.

"Every word is the truth. You're pitiful, Tazman. Four years of war and you still know nothing. Now, sit down, and I'll tell you everything I know." He did not move. "Sit down!"

He relented. She took another draw on her cigarette, exhaled. "Bugloss is the city's most revered *xiao jie*. You do know what a *xiao jie* is, right? Good, then you're not that naive."

"How do you know this?"

"I saw her once at a comfort station, with the other women. It was a few years ago. But when you came to me and asked about her, I thought I'd start there. And what do you know? The place still exists. It's no longer a comfort station, of course. But that's just a different name for what it is. I asked around. Remember Violet? She was here when you last saw me? She told me about that place, and about Bugloss. Oh, yes, Bugloss. Back when the Japanese were here, she was the lieutenant's favorite. Week after week the lieutenant visited her, and they stayed in their room for hours. And now, men want Bugloss. Men can't have Bugloss, at least not without a fistful of cash. That was why I told you to get the money. You wouldn't have had a chance without it."

"You're such a liar."

"Why would I lie to you?"

"Because you're jealous."

Her cackles were bitter and amused at the same time. "Don't flatter yourself. I have men who give me things, all kinds of things. Pretty things. See this silk robe? This gold ring? They spoil me. I have everything I want. Why should I be jealous? She means nothing to me."

"Then why didn't you just tell me?"

"It was better for you to find out yourself. It's none of my business. Not really. And you know what? I don't really give a damn. You should leave."

"What about Grace?"

"What about her? You already know where to find her. It's your problem now. And our conversation is over." She stubbed out her cigarette. "Madam," she yelled. "Madam!"

He did not wait for Chin to show up. He had to get out of this hole. Away from this place. Away from Mei's desperate lies.

He went back to the east quadrant and waited on the street. Occasionally a man or two would enter the row house, and different men would leave. He waited until he ran out of time. He returned to the shoe shop and buried himself in its never-ending tasks.

ᘓᘓTHE ENDᘓᘓ

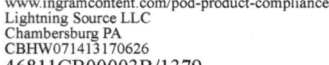